With Best wishes to Sarah.

THE
FRENCH
EMPEROR'S
WOMAN

The
French
Emperor's
Woman

David Bissenden

Matador
9 Priory Business Park,
Wistow Road, Kibworth Beauchamp,
Leicestershire. LE8 0RX
Tel: 0116 279 2299
Email: books@troubador.co.uk
Web: www.troubador.co.uk/matador
Twitter: @matadorbooks

ISBN 978 1800461 444

British Library Cataloguing in Publication Data.
A catalogue record for this book is available from the British Library.

Printed and bound in Great Britain by 4edge Limited
Typeset in 11pt Adobe Garamond Pro by Troubador Publishing Ltd, Leicester, UK

Matador is an imprint of Troubador Publishing Ltd

To my wife Jane, for her forbearance

PART 1

In the Shadow of Waterloo

ONE

Crimea

IT WAS JUNE 18TH, 1855. I remember that day well, as it was exactly forty years on from the glorious victory at Waterloo. As a child I had been brought up on stories of the bravery of our troops in the Napoleonic Wars, the battle plans, victories, and triumphs. Now, aged twenty-four, I was here in person, fighting for Her Majesty, Queen Victoria. I, William Arthur Reeves – a Royal Engineer, in a far distant land.

I had joined the sappers back in 1852, just days after the death of the Duke of Wellington, with dreams of emulating his success. I was sure that a military career was for me; now I was in Crimea facing Russian troops in a bloody conflict.

We were positioned just outside Sevastopol, a town we had laid siege to for several months. Today was to have been the big push to take the town and give the Russians a bloody nose. Sadly, at this moment in time all was not going to plan. Our advances were being met by a hail of gunfire, with grapeshot from their cannon exploding all around us; tearing chunks out of grown men, making them cry like babies and weep for their mothers. Shrapnel goes everywhere, in your belly, your legs, ripping half of your face off – if it caught you right. You almost longed for a clean bullet through the heart or head. A clean end to all this.

I was hurting, something had hit my upper leg; hard, right down in the thighbone. I did not want to look, hopefully just a musket ball had glanced off it. Lucky really, it could just as easily have hit my head, but I could not move my leg anymore, so I knew that my presence on the battlefield was now pointless. I had become a liability, but retreat was not an option. So, I just lay in the mud, literally keeping my head down.

Time passed but my predicament was not improving, the pain in my leg was worsening as the initial shock wore off. Then as fear and pain tired me, one of our own, Charlie Gordon, appeared to my right and crouched down beside me.

'Everything alright Reeves?'

'Thigh looks like it's caught something – bloody useless,' I replied. Gordon was unfazed.

'No problem, just crawl back to our first position, get it dressed. I'll vouch for you if there's any trouble.'

I looked back at him gratefully. Gordon was a cool customer, never seemed upset by anything, very brave in the face of fire. Some thought he was too brave, almost as if he had a death wish. But he was my saviour that day.

'Alright,' I said through clenched teeth, and started crawling back.

After a while, the crawl became a limping walk and within minutes, I was back at the wagons, where there might be a chance of receiving medical help. At that point, the reality of the day hit me. The few medical orderlies were totally overwhelmed by casualties. Men with limbs hanging off, and open stomach wounds. A scene of carnage. It was obvious that they would not have time for me. Almost embarrassed by my petty wound, I slunk away, using my rifle as a crutch. I found a dry area by an ammunition cart and positioned myself with my back against the wheels. I just sat there, with my bloodied leg straight in front of me, staring into space and hoping the pain would go away.

It was not long before I could hear a soft moaning from inside the cart itself. With difficulty I pulled myself up and using both hands to support my weight grasped the top of the timber side and peered over to look into it. The sight that greeted me made my hair stand on end. Lying in an almost foetal position on the timber planking of the cart was a wounded British drummer boy. Perhaps no more than fifteen. He was in full uniform with bright madder red jacket and white trousers, but from his chest down, his body was covered in his own blood and gore. I could see at a glance he would not make it. The grapeshot, or whatever, had torn his stomach open from his heart to below the navel. It was an odious sight and I could see the unbearable pain he was in. I think he was calling for his mother, his ma, but I could not be sure. Slowly his head moved, and his eyes caught mine. A look of total disbelief, pain, and incredulity was written all over his face. He stared for a few moments, mouthed the words 'Kill me', then his eyes closed momentarily. I looked back at him. There was absolutely no way he was going to live. So, I did my duty. I picked up my discarded rifle; took off the long bayonet, then pointed it at the drummer boy's head. I knew my fate was to dispatch him in one clean shot, and I did this. Just before I pulled the trigger, his eyes met mine and for a brief instant – he stared at me. Then he gave the gentlest of nods. I fired; the bullet smashed through his forehead and he was gone.

At that point I realised how awful and pointless it all was. I understood for the first time just how bloody disgusting war is. In the textbooks you read battles are glorious intellectual exercises, your troops against theirs, strategy, positioning, cunning – all would help you get the upper hand. Here, though, on the ground today, was the reality. Blood, smell, cries for mother, flies everywhere – all happening in a war we barely understood. A war badly organised and prepared for, where your army clothes were not designed for the weather, your rations insufficient for your needs, and even your weaponry and ammunition were not fit for purpose.

I decided there and then that if I were ever to get out of this Russian hell and back to England, I would leave the army and go into politics to try and stop wars, and if that were not possible, to make sure our armies were properly equipped, fed, watered and looked after, if sick or injured in battle.

Finally, at day's end, with the light fading, our orderlies had time to sort out my injury. Nobody asked what had happened to the drummer boy. They might have guessed. I watched as his body was taken away for a rudimentary burial in a freshly dug communal trench. How I would have liked to get his details and contacted his mother to tell her how brave he was, but I did not.

The leg was not too bad. It got bandaged, so the bleeding stopped. I was now one of the walking wounded and was led down to the port of Balaclava in a column of other wounded and sick men; I would have been happy to have been evacuated back to England, but no ships were available, so I stayed, the wound healed enough for me to resume my duties. I was in Crimea for another year, braving the horrendous winter, and the mud of the thaw in spring. Finally, our regiment sailed back to England and not long after that I left the Royal Engineers and returned to live in my brother's rooms in London. Like so many other veterans, I was now looking for a new life.

TWO

My Mission

I HAD DREAMED OF POLITICS but soon found out that was a rich man's profession. You had to be wealthy or well connected, or ideally both. So instead I became a journalist, often investigating stories of the maimed and broken men who had come back from the war in Crimea and were now penniless. Often these men had become separated from their families and were living on the streets.

Strangely it was this philanthropic activity that ended up as my major source of income. I discovered that there were thousands of missing people in London and almost as many relatives and friends looking for them. With my knowledge of this world, I was able to secure some income from tracking down these lost people, as a kind of unofficial private detective. I never advertised this fact but by word of mouth I had any number of clients seeking their lost ones. I also secured a regular column in a weekly newspaper, so all in all, I was not doing too badly. My only sadness was that I had never felt financially secure enough to marry, so at forty was still a bachelor. Essentially, I lived a modest life, on modest income, still living with my brother George, who worked in the printing industry at Fleet Street. We shared small rooms on the Whitechapel Road, just east of the city.

It came as some surprise to me then, when on a Saturday morning in the summer of 1871, a letter came through my door from Charles Gordon. He was now famous for his role in the Chinese rebellions of the late 1850s and had the nickname 'Chinese Gordon'. The letter came from Gravesend, which is where he was stationed as the commissioner for rebuilding the Thames forts. He had also earned a reputation as a philanthropist, helping the poor, underfed children of Gravesend through the church and schools.

I was even more surprised to see from the letter that he remembered me from Crimea and wanted to meet to discuss a confidential matter, at his office in New Tavern Fort, Gravesend on the Monday.

I was delighted to know he had not forgotten me. On the Monday I duly caught the train from Fenchurch Street to Tilbury and got the ferry over to Gravesend. It was a fine summer day and the river was full of traffic making its way along the river to and from London. Many of the ships were colliers, and other cargo carriers, taking their goods to the capital city. There were also heavily loaded barges, with large blood-red sails stretched in the wind, taking hay to feed the working horses of the city, and then bringing the manure back out to the farms along the estuary.

Gravesend itself was a busy port and the main point of Customs and Excise clearance on the River Thames for London.

It was a few minutes' walk from the ferry stage to the fort. I passed the Three Daws public house and the Clarendon Hotel, before reaching the gatehouse of New Tavern Fort. I introduced myself to the guard on duty and was escorted through the building to Gordon's office. All around me it was obvious that the fort was being rebuilt, with building materials, scaffolding, and stone masons everywhere.

Rounding a bend in the fort walls, I could see Gordon straight ahead of me – standing in the doorway. He had not changed that much since I had last seen him fifteen years ago. Though not tall, perhaps five feet and a half, he had a presence about him. There was still the crisp moustache and tight curly hair, piercing blue eyes, a steely gaze, and a stern military posture, all finished off with a Royal Engineer's uniform. He spoke first.

'Good to see you again Reeves. Come on in.'

Without any more chitchat he summoned me into what I presume was his office. Typically for Gordon it was an austere affair. No pictures of his military triumphs, no awards, or medals, just a desk and two seats.

'Come, take a seat Reeves. Good journey?'

I smiled. 'Very good sir, and I'm most impressed by the works here.'

He took this compliment in his stride.

'Indeed, I'd rather be abroad myself but needs must.'

He sat down, I did likewise. 'Well,' he said, 'I believe it is sixteen years since we last met. It was at the battle of Sevastopol, June 18th, 1855 – if my memory serves me well.' He smiled slightly but I sensed that he was not one for idle conversation.

'It is indeed, and you have become a true British hero since then – Chinese Gordon the press call you, whilst I have just been keeping my head above water by writing and finding lost persons.'

Gordon adjusted his posture slightly.

'Indeed. Now, as you know Reeves, I am not one for small talk, never have been. I have called you because a problem has been presented to me, one that I cannot solve alone. Obviously, everything I tell you about this problem must remain strictly confidential?'

'Of course.'

'Good, I wouldn't expect anything other than that.' He drummed the table with his fingernails, then continued.

'I had a visit last week from an envoy, working on behalf of Louis Napoleon – or Napoleon III as he likes to be called, who is living in exile at Camden Place in Chislehurst – about ten miles from here. Obviously, this was awkward for me as you are probably aware that the reconstruction of these forts was instigated by fears of French expansionism in the first place. As luck would have it, we are halfway through the works and France is no longer a threat to anyone, as they were thoroughly beaten in their war against Prussia. However, one issue that came out of that war was the potential for French refugees fleeing the conflict coming to England, particularly those caught up in the siege of Paris. Are you still with me?'

'Of course.'

It appears that Napoleon is in some way connected to a child, a thirteen -year- old , named Pierre Le Beau. Pierre and his mother , who was also once, the lady-in-waiting to the Empress Eugenie ,was stuck in Paris after the defeat at Sedan at the beginning of September. The Empress had already left the Tuileries in Paris secretly, and via Deauville sailed over to England, arriving on the south coast on the 8th September. A few days later Pierre, and his mother Marie-Anne, left Paris and reached the port of Rouen on the lower Seine. Now, Marie-Anne wanted to go and support Louis Napoleon, rather than join Eugenie in England, so she arranged for Pierre to be put aboard the *Spirit of Rochester*, which was docked in Rouen, and en route to London. Meanwhile she travelled alone by train to Brussels where she had some discussion with the French Ambassador. From there she travelled east and joined Napoleon's court, which was effectively imprisoned at Cassell in central Germany. So far so good. Pierre was due to arrive on September 18th at the pool of London. The problem was – he never arrived. Some members of the French embassy were waiting at Trinity House by the Tower, but when the ship docked there was no sign of him. The only other stopping place after leaving Rouen was Gravesend, for Customs clearance. Again no one saw him leave the ship, but –and this is the interesting thing – there was a rumour that at nightfall, when the *Spirit* was moored outside the town on the Hope, a rowing boat left the ship and brought someone ashore. Now, it appears that somehow this rumour got back to Napoleon's court. They have since tried to trace Pierre through Scotland Yard and the Kent constabulary, but got nowhere. So, hearing that I have dealings with lost boys through my school here in Gravesend, they came to ask if I had come across him or had heard any rumours of his whereabouts.' He paused for breath.

'Unfortunately, I've nothing to help them. I have made enquiries but got nowhere. Also, it is of course somewhat awkward for a commander in the Royal Engineers to be actively helping a French emperor in exile. That is where you come in – you are experienced in finding lost people. I also know you can be trusted implicitly. So, I am asking. Can you help me with this issue?'

I looked straight back at Gordon and replied without hesitation.

'Of course, I will do all I can – but where is our starting point? What clues do we have?'

Gordon stared solemnly ahead. 'Precious little I'm afraid, the only lead is this sighting of a rowing boat coming ashore from the boat. I can give you the details of the person who says they saw this. That is all I have. Of course, the constabulary have interviewed the captain of the *Spirit of Rochester*, John Lynch, but he denies everything. He did not stowaway the boy. Has never heard of him. Knows nothing.' I sighed; this was not going to be easy, but I owed it to Gordon to help.

'Alright then, I'm happy to help in any way I can. Can you give me the details of the person who saw the rowing boat?'

Gordon smiled.

'Yes, indeed. His name is Jack Carter, or One-legged Jack, as he is more commonly known. He lives up on the hill overlooking the town. He is an old sea captain himself and spends half his time spying on the river with a powerful telescope. Keeps a log of everything he sees. The Customs boys have found him useful in the past. This sighting was just one entry on his log but coincides with the time and location of the *Spirit* being moored on the Hope. Another tip: take a bottle of brandy with you, he probably has some gossip that might come in useful. Here's his address, just up the hill from here.'

And that was that. No mention of payment for my work, but then Gordon did not think on that level. A child was missing, it was our Christian duty to find him.

'I think I will need to stay in Gravesend for a few days to get to grips with this, I assume you will not want me staying here at the Fort?'

Charles was clearly non-plussed that I should ask such a stupid question.

'Certainly not, I don't want it to be known that I have any connection to this investigation. Your presence here is purely to be thought of as an old friend, an old army pal, meeting up – I suggest you stay at the Eagle on West Street, it is quite cheap and is close to the seamen's pubs. It is right by the river, but I suggest you get a room overlooking the street, as you will sleep better away from the boats on the river – which are surprisingly noisy, even at night. I will pay your bills for now and in addition a retainer of two pounds per week. We understand each other?'

I concurred with him that this seemed a satisfactory arrangement and prepared to leave.

Gordon bade me adieu at his office door. Although we had not spoken for over fifteen years, he made no effort to prolong the conversation.

I walked out past the sentry and into a warm Gravesend afternoon with a gentle breeze blowing off the river. This was indeed one of the most difficult assignments I had ever taken on, but my loyalty to Gordon and intrigue about the whole affair made it impossible to resist.

THREE

Settling into Gravesend

I IMMEDIATELY CALLED INTO THE Eagle and organised my lodgings – I could go home for some belongings later. The publican, Sam, showed me up to my room on the second floor. It was a modest affair but clearly the hotel was of reasonable quality and catered for a slightly better class of travelling salesman and the like; in short the room was perfectly adequate for my needs. It also had a decent view down West Street. For those of you who do not know Gravesend, let me give you a brief description of the view from my bedroom. The Eagle was situated at the west end of West Street. Looking to the east you would see a brewery warehouse and beyond that the King's Arms inn. Then a few more commercial properties and you reached the Three Daws inn, which was next to the town's ferry stage and opposite the north end of the high street. The high street climbed away from the river towards the town centre. Along the street, about 200 yards up, were the town hall and courtroom beside the marketplace. At the far southern end of the high street was Gravesend railway station. Coming back to the Three Daws, if you carried on along the riverside to the east you reached the Clarendon Hotel, followed by the Customs and Excise building, and just beyond that, New Tavern Fort itself.

It was a busy little town and often the first port for ships coming up the Thames to London, hence the importance of the Customs House for checking incoming boats. The river trade had made the town wealthier, but it still had some dodgy riverside drinking dens, which gave it an air of excitement and unpredictability.

I could not give myself any more time to linger over my thoughts, there was work to be done, and quickly. I decided to heed Gordon's advice and arm myself with a bottle of brandy, so walked into the nearest pub, the King's Arms, not far from the ferry landing stage. Not the most salubrious place. Sawdust floor, several very drunken old timers with swollen red and purple noses at the bar. It struck me as the kind of place where bad business could be done at will.

I quickly purchased the brandy from the bemused publican – clearly, I was not his usual sort of customer – and walked out into the street. I was very struck by the difference in the atmosphere inside, and outside the inn. Gravesend was a prosperous town with a train station, shops, good housing; all the attributes of well-ordered Victorian life, but inside the pub was a different world. A place of old seamen, danger, and dark secrets. I could imagine that illegal dealing of goods, and prostitution, would be easily to hand. The dark and light sides of England, just yards apart.

I walked up the hill and quickly found the terrace of cottages. The end one was where Jack Carter lived. It was a modest affair but benefited from unobstructed views of the river. One day new houses would be built nearby, and that view would be gone but for now it had a panorama of the river and the ship movements occurring on it.

I knocked on the door and waited. Finally, an old man dressed in a thick pullover, with a gammy leg, sucking on a long, cream-coloured clay pipe came to the door.

'Yes,' he said gruffly.

'Hello, let me introduce myself, my name is William Reeves and I'm a writer and journalist. I'm writing a book about seafaring in Gravesend and I was wondering if you could help me with my research?'

He looked me up and down. 'So how do you know about me?'

'I've made some feelers in the town and everyone says that Jack Carter, who lives on the hill, is the man to ask about Gravesend and the stories of old-time seafaring.' He seemed to brighten up at this.

'So, what do you want exactly?' he said.

'Just a conversation to get snippets of local life for my book.' I took the brandy out of my coat pocket. 'I thought this might oil the wheels of your memory?'

He smiled. 'Come on in.'

He led me through his cottage, which was jam-packed with memorabilia of his sea-going days. Even the walls of the rooms seemed to be lined with timber planking that may have once been part of boats he sailed in. He bade me to sit down in an armchair opposite his. He also opened his drinks cabinet and brought out two crystal glasses. Getting the cue, I had soon half-filled these. We sat down. I thought I would try and get him in a cordial mood so started with some small talk.

"This is a fine house – I've never seen so much maritime history and artefacts in one place. Is it all yours?'

Jack smiled.

'Collected over many years. My father and his father were seafarers. Even my only son, Tom, went to sea for a while. Was on the spice runs from India. Poor lad got malaria off the Gold Coast and was taken ashore at Freetown to die.' I could see his hurt on that one.

'Sorry to hear that. The oceans can be a dangerous place.'

He sniffed. 'You have to be a mariner to know just how dangerous they can be. Anyway – what is it you want exactly?'

'I am really just trying to find out about what life was like for a sea-going man back in the Napoleon's time. How the town has changed, and so on.'

He grunted and with measured words replied, 'I can tell you a thousand and one stories about this place, a lot from the past when we had press gangs, and smuggling was rife. I can tell you stories from today as well.' He took a drag from the glass then a quick puff on his pipe, then continued. 'Thing is, what people don't know is that things haven't changed as much as you think. I know the high street is full of gents wearing suits and bowler hats going to the station, catching trains up to town, and ladies sitting in hansom cabs and the like, but behind all that if you go down into the riverside pubs, late at night, you'll see a different world. Men so drunk they cannot stand, whores working down the alleyways, bottles of brandy and the like being slipped off boats when the Customs aren't looking. And that's not the half of it.' He carried on in this vein for a long, long time. Clearly, he did not have many visitors these days and was only to happy to share his thoughts with anyone interested in them.

I wanted to try and gently prise some relevant information from him, so I asked, "Talking about characters, are there any really dangerous seafarers still in Gravesend? You know, people you wouldn't want to cross?'

He thought for a moment. 'So many of them. Tommy Tibbalds is one; he runs the boat-breaking yard at Denton. There's more on the wrong side of the law, than the right side.'

'What about sea captains who visit the town, any bad ones?'

'Well, I've not been to sea for a few years now but the ones who were bad 'uns then who are still about now are the same. Let me think.' He paused to gather his thoughts. 'Probably Lynchy is the worst.'

'Lynch?'

'Yea, John Lynch, captain of the *Spirit of Rochester*. I was mates with him once, a long time ago. He even got a job on board for my boy Tom, but I have fallen out with him since. If you have any dealings with him, keep your wits about you. He is into all sorts. Or so they say. Thing is I don't mind a bit of people smuggling or fiddling the Excise duty. It is the sex thing that upsets me.' He puffed even more fervently on his clay pipe.

'What do you mean?'

'Sex, you know, paying for it or not as the case may be. Now I've no problem with paying the whores round here.

That is just business, if you get a dose of the clap, so be it, but some of the sailors are worse than that. They get their way with boys, some not even twelve. Now that is wrong, that is.'

I replied quickly. 'That is terrible, and of course it's a criminal offence.'

He scoffed. 'Only if you're caught.'

'So, are you saying this Captain Lynch and his crew have got a taste for boys, when they're ashore?' There was an awkward pause. He seemed to come to his senses suddenly.

'I'm not saying anything about anyone. I think you have had enough today. What's this all about anyway?'

I cleared my throat. 'The truth is Jack; I'm looking for a boy who has been lost. Who has disappeared off the face of the earth. The only clue I have is that he may have come ashore in a rowing boat on the night of the 17th September last year. I believe you made a note in your log of a rowing boat coming from the '*Spirit of Rochester*' around midnight. Just a boy being rowed by two men.?'

He got to his feet, clearly flustered. 'I just keep a log on what I see from my bedroom window. I don't want no eavesdropper putting two and two together and getting me in trouble. Now, be on your way.'

Clearly, he was terribly upset, so I made my way to the door and stepped out. He virtually slammed the door behind me. Perhaps I had handled that badly, but it did seem from what was said, that indeed Captain Lynch was as rotten as a pear and perfectly capable of kidnapping the French boy.

I walked back down to the town. What was to be done now? Having concerns about someone, and being able to prove it, were two different things. And if Pierre had come ashore where was he being hidden? Where to start looking?

FOUR

Searching

FOR THE NEXT FEW DAYS I stayed in the town, residing at the Eagle. My room had a view out over the busy street, and I could see and hear workers from the nearby brewery, coming and going to work. Early morning the drays left the yard, loaded up with barrels of beer, their heavy horses' hoofs clattering over the granite setts, with their drayman talking loudly to each other and anyone else awake at this early hour. Also, every day ;a strange-looking man with a heavy black leather briefcase and a pronounced limp, using a stick, walked from the brewery offices, down West Street towards Town Pier – and ten minutes later he returned. Same time every day, to the minute. There was also the milkman and the baker doing their rounds, in fact the hustle and bustle never stopped. All in all, a noisy affair, guaranteed to wake you up.

During the day I walked the town, getting to know its nooks and crannies. Often, I would visit the riverside pubs in the hope of overhearing some nugget of information, but nothing. Clearly, I was an outsider and was treated as such.

The seamen who frequented the alehouses kept themselves to themselves. It was a dispiriting experience.

On the third day I received a message from Gordon, he needed to see me. I immediately and briskly strode down to his office at the fort. I was ushered in straight away. Gordon sat by his desk and bade me sit down without any small talk or greeting.

Gordon took his hands from behind his head and reached across the desk towards me.

'Have you had any success with your investigations?'

I looked sheepish as I replied, 'I'm afraid that little progress had been made. My meeting with Jack Carter was useful but the seafaring community who might have some knowledge of what occurred are tight lipped and appear to be a closed shop where outsiders cannot find out anything.'

He looked at me with clear disappointment in his eyes.

'So, what can we do Reeves?, How can we break into this web of silence?'

I thought for a moment then taking my courage in both hands, broached the issue that I knew Gordon would be awkward on.

'It could be that the kidnappers, for that's what they are, have one Achilles heel. From talking to Jack, I got the impression that Lynch has a taste for, shall we say, his own kind.'

Gordon looked perplexed.

'What do you mean, Reeves?'

I could feel his discomfiture but carried on.

'The inference is, from my talk with Carter, that Lynch may have homosexual tendencies, he may have a taste for younger men. In fact, boys.'

Gordon's face turned red with rage.

'How dare you mention such unspeakable behaviour. How dare you bring these disgusting thoughts and theories into this office.'

There was an awkward silence before I continued.

'I appreciate this is disgusting, ungodly behaviour, but in real life it does go on, and if true, might be Lynch's undoing. Can you honestly say that in your dealings with the poor children at the ragged school, you did not hear of such rumours?'

Gordon was uncomfortable but defiant.

'Yes, I heard such rumours, but the thought is so repugnant that I dispelled them as pure gossip.' The meeting was getting awkward, but I had to continue.

'I'm sorry sir, but I cannot crack this case unless I can get down to the nitty gritty. Now, were there any boys that you know might have indulged in this behaviour —albeit they may have been forced into it by callous and bestial older men?'

Gordon sighed. 'Alright, I will speak to the housekeeper of the school and ask if they have any boys who might have been damaged in this way.'

I felt, finally, that progress was being made.

'Thank you.'

Gordon clearly now wanted to move on to more comfortable territory. He reached down and picked up a telegram lying on his desk. 'Meanwhile I have a request for you; a lady-in-waiting at Napoleon's court , Marie-Anne, is coming to Gravesend tomorrow and will be staying at the Clarendon Hotel. She would like to meet you for tea at three o'clock to discuss progress. Can you do that?'

'Of course.'

'Very well, see yourself out and keep me informed of any progress, and be cautious with Marie-Anne, I believe she is close to Napoleon, and was once his mistress. So be careful what you say and do. As you may know, the Emperor is in Victoria's good books now, so any mistake by you could have consequences. Do we understand each other?'

'Of course,' I replied, and walked out of the room.

FIVE

The Meeting

AT THE APPOINTED HOUR I arrived at the Clarendon, a fine brick-built building that overlooked the Thames. It was regarded as the best hotel in town and had benefited greatly from a visit by the Prince of Wales, a few years earlier.

I walked in though the main doorway and then headed for the dining room, which was well signposted. I could see at once that the hotel was of a good standard. The dining room boasted deep red velvet curtains, cheerful in summer and warm in winter. Hanging from the white plaster ceiling, decorated at the centre by rose fittings, were crystal chandeliers with integral gaslights. The tables were dark mahogany set off by pristine white table clothes. Each table had a decorative table lamp with a weighted porcelain figure. Even the silver sugar bowls were covered by Belgian lace.

At what looked to be the best table in the room – overlooking the green down to the river – was a very elegant lady. She had her maid in attendance, a slightly older, less attractive woman. I walked over to the table and bowed deeply.

'Madame Marie, so pleased to meet you, I am William Reeves, at your service.' She took my hand lightly, just the fingertips, and nodded.

'Thank you Mr Reeves for coming at such short notice. This is my maid, Antonia.' She gestured to the older women at her side, who had very stern features beneath obviously dyed jet-black hair. Antonia curtseyed deeply but all the talking was done by Marie.

'Please take a seat so we can get down to business.' I obeyed her wishes without question; she had authority as well as beauty.

'Antonia. You can take your leave of us now.' At that the maid curtseyed more deeply and departed, leaving me alone with Marie. I quickly took stock of the lady. Her immediate impact was pronounced; she had a real elegance about her. Probably in her middle thirties, she was a beauty with piercing brown eyes and dark hair tied into a bun, tucked within a bonnet. She perched rather than sat on her chair, and I detected a lovely smell of lemon and bergamot perfume exuding from her. She was wearing one of the modern colours – a deep shade of maroon, and her outfit was fringed with white lacework. She was unsmiling, but this took nothing away from her presence in the room. She spoke in perfect English with scarcely a trace of a French accent.

'Let me first say how grateful I am for your assistance in this matter, you were recommended to me by Lieutenant-Colonel Gordon, who is a fine man. I must also say, this is a matter of great sensitivity. As you are aware Emperor

Napoleon has only been living in your country for three months and that is due to the kindness of your government and Queen Victoria, so we must be discreet in all our activities. Do you understand?'

I replied without hesitation. 'Yes, all matters discussed will be completely confidential.'

She continued. 'You have been briefed about the kidnap?'

'Yes.' She seemed content at this and relaxed.

'Would you like some tea William? Is it alright to call you William?'

'Yes, of course.' She reached for the teapot and after pouring out a cup, she dispensed some milk and sugar into it deftly. All her movements were measured and elegant. She cleared her throat.

'Very well. I appreciate we have little to go on at the moment, just a report that Pierre may have been taken off the *Spirit of Rochester* before it reached Gravesend, but I am so desperate for answers to this, that I have come to the town to see if there are any further clues as to his whereabouts.'

I looked at her. She was clearly distressed but too refined and self-contained to show her emotions outwardly. I decided to ask the awkward question at once.

'Of course, I understand the sensitivity of this, but firstly I must enquire: is the missing boy Pierre your son?'

'Yes,' she replied without hesitation. I knew at this point my feeble efforts so far would disappoint but continued anyway.

'Thank you for being candid with me on that issue. I am sorry to say that though I have been in Gravesend for a few days, following Gordon's intervention, I have made little progress. I will keep trying of course but up to now there have been no obvious leads.'

She was clearly disappointed. 'What about the captain of the boat, this John Lynch. Have you spoken to him?'

'I am afraid he is presently at sea but should be back in Gravesend in the next few days. My understanding is that he has denied everything – picking Pierre up in Rouen, stowing him away illegally – everything. He says he has no idea who Pierre is, and no boy was picked up at Rouen.'

She scowled at this. 'The man is a liar! My people arranged this with him and paid him good money. He is liar and a thief.'

I felt her anger but knew I must keep my feelings in check, so I replied in a measured tone.

'That may well be true but in English law we have to prove it. I will endeavour to find Pierre by any means possible and that may require interviewing Lynch at some stage.'

She was clearly not impressed.

'In the French empire we know how to get the truth out of people. How do you think we conquered Algeria and Indo China? By being nice?'

I was flummoxed slightly but carried on.

'I understand your impatience, but we cannot do that in this country.'

She sighed then smiled. It was the first time I had seen that expression. It was like watching the sun touch the winter snow, seeing her smile, and to me revealed a wholly different person hidden under this veil of anger and propriety.

'It is a great shame we cannot extract the truth, but I know that here in England we are guests of your country, we have to be careful how we behave. We must be like the British, stiff upper lip and all that. So, what do you suggest we should do?'

This was the question I was worried about, as I knew no answer of mine would satisfy her.

'I have a line of enquiry I'm following through contacts of Gordon but that may take time. The only other proposal I have is to somehow meet Lynch when he is next in port. If the Customs office will help with this, it should be possible.'

'What about the Kent *gendarme*... I mean constabulary. Surely they can help.'

I had to consciously stop shrugging at this point.

'I believe they have spoken to Lynch and got the usual story – that he knows nothing. Without firm evidence they will not arrest him, so I'm afraid they are of little use to us at this point.'

I searched my brain for some kernel of hope. 'What I can do is arrange a meeting with the Excise office. I am sure Gordon will give me an entrée into that. Also, are there any pictures of Pierre available?' She looked over her shoulder and clicked her fingers. The maid reappeared with a box. Passed it to her, curtsied, then left.

'I have a photograph of the family, taken in 1869, so it is fairly recent. Here you are.' She passed over a picture of a family group; there was only one boy in it, so I knew it must be Pierre. The family group was Pierre, Marie, and a man in uniform. I studied the picture.

'Who is this gentleman?'

She was clearly vexed at me asking the question.

'The man in the picture is the head of the Emperor's household, Monsieur Matthew Toulouse. We brought him into the frame so that it looks like a normal family photograph and nothing to perturb the photographer, or anyone else seeing the picture.' I looked it over; while obviously formal and two years old, it was still of a good quality.

'Can I borrow this and get a lithograph print made of Pierre? I may need to make a direct appeal to the public by displaying his picture where people can see it, perhaps pinning it onto trees and the like, with a plea as to anyone knowing his whereabouts. Is that alright?' She thought for a moment.

'Very well. But please, be careful with the picture. It is all I have left of my son.'

This was clearly a delicate situation.

'I fully understand and promise to take good care of it. Now for the wording below the picture. What about "Pierre Le Beau, French national aged thirteen, travelled to Gravesend 17th September 1870, but not seen since. Anybody with information as to his whereabouts pleases contact William Reeves, care of Eagle Hotel, West Street, Gravesend. Information which leads to his discovery will be rewarded".' I paused to see her reaction. She nodded.

'Yes, that is fine. I will leave that in your hands then.' She sat back and for a moment seemed to relax before speaking. I sensed our meeting had run its course, and she confirmed this with her next words.

'Shall we meet again, here tomorrow at the same time to discuss progress?'

'Yes, good idea. Obviously if any other information comes to hand, I will contact you immediately.'

'*Merci,*' she responded.

At that I stood up, bowed deeply, and left the restaurant with her precious photograph tucked under my arm.

SIX

Meetings with Men
of Importance

AFTER LEAVING THE CLARENDON, I immediately returned to
the fort to see Gordon. He was as terse as ever, but I managed
to get from him the address of a good local lithographer and
a letter of introduction to the Chief Clerk of Customs and
Excise.

Armed with this, I visited Gordon's chosen printer. He was
happy to do the work, so I left the photograph in his hands.

I then walked to the Excise office. This was a fairly new
and impressive red brick building, close to the riverside and
only yards from the fort. I passed over Gordon's letter at
the reception, and after a longer wait than was comfortable
was shown in to see the Chief Clerk, a Mr Atkins. He was
a well-dressed fellow and clearly by the size of his desk, was
an important person within the Excise office. He was bald
and wore spectacles, over which he looked at me as I entered
the room.

He greeted me with a firm handshake and a well-rehearsed but curt salutation.

'Good afternoon. Tom Atkins – Her Majesty's Chief Customs Officer, Gravesend. Please, take a seat. Now, how can I help you Mr Reeves?'

I sat down and began my story.

'Firstly, let me thank you Mr Atkins for taking time out to see me. My business is regarding a French citizen, a thirteen-year-old boy name of Pierre Le Beau. He boarded the British ship the *Spirit of Rochester* in Rouen on September 16th last year. Sailing to London via Gravesend. He was due in the port of London on the 18th September, but never arrived. However, rumour has it that a boy was seen on a rowing boat, leaving the *Spirit* off Gravesend the night before, so he may have been brought ashore without your knowledge.'

I sat forward and tried to give more weight to my final sentence. 'Obviously, if that is so, it would be a situation of interest to you.'

Atkins reached for a polished brown wooden pipe that sat to the left side of his desk, and after a few taps, lit it, and brought it to his mouth.

'Mr Reeves, I am aware of all of this, and I'm sure you mean well. However, the *Spirit of Rochester*'s captain denies all knowledge of this, and says he knows nothing about picking up this boy in Rouen or bringing him ashore in Gravesend. I am afraid this is all speculation and hearsay. So, I cannot be of any help I fear.'

At this my spirits dropped, this is what I had been told to expect, but somehow I still had hoped for something more.

'Is there anything that could help my investigations in this matter?' Atkins looked me up and down before speaking slowly and in measured tones.

'The only thing that may be worth pursuing is to speak to the boat's shipping agents. They are Bennett and Sons, who are based near Billingsgate Market in the City. If your story is true, then somebody must have paid the captain to take on board a stowaway, and the possible path for those monies might be via the agent.'

I was grateful for this, at least I could now report back to Marie with something. 'Thank you. I'll make haste to their offices in the city now.' Atkins smiled thinly. 'No need to go so far, Mr Reeves. They have their own agent here in Gravesend, John Bennett is his name. He has an office down on West Street, on the first floor of the brewery warehouse. You can't miss him; he walks with a pronounced limp.' I was delighted at this news and thanked Mr Atkins warmly.

'Good luck,' he said. 'I think you're going to need it in this case.'

I shook his hand, walked back through the building, and emerged out into the street, which was warmed by the late afternoon sunshine.

For some reason instinct told me not to immediately visit John Bennett at the brewery. So, I spent the rest of the day trying to piece together what I had discovered to date. Clearly there were still many missing pieces from the jigsaw. I needed more time but that might not be available.

Next day, I walked to the lithographers where I collected the foolscap size posters of Pierre. With the addition of drawing pins, bought from a corner shop, I was soon putting the poster on every available tree and timber building I could find. Luckily, it was a fine sunny day, so this was not that tiresome a task. This filled in most of the morning and before I knew it, the time was 3 p.m. and I was back at the Clarendon.

SEVEN

The Emperor's Woman

I WALKED IN AND COULD see Marie-Anne at her usual table, although Antonia sat opposite her. There seemed little warmth or talk between them. However instead of beckoning me to sit down, she had other ideas.

'Hello, William. I wonder if we could go for a walk. The weather is wonderful, and this hotel gets so stuffy. Antonia, you can stay here.' She smiled. I was only too happy to agree.

We left the hotel by the front door, side by side. To any spectator we looked like an affluent middle-class couple on a private visit to the riverside resort. I could not help but feel privileged that such a beautiful lady was willing to walk alongside me, even if only in the pursuit of a professional matter.

We strolled over to the riverside and she looked out over the waters towards Tilbury Fort on the north bank. Despite the constant movement of boats, the river had a great charm that seemed to have affected Marie.

'This is quite a nice place. It reminds me a little of Paris, or perhaps Rouen, with the River Seine flowing past.' She smiled at me. 'It is a pleasant spot and if we were not engaged on such awful business, I could enjoy this very much.' Pleasantries over, her face hardened. 'Now tell me what progress have you made?'

I briefly told her of the posters being displayed around town, and my meeting with the Excise office. However, I could tell from her body language that she was clearly disappointed at the lack of progress so far.

'William, this is becoming very frustrating – we are not getting any closer to Pierre's whereabouts, are we?'

I had to agree with her but bade her to be patient and hope the posters might yield some information. I also knew I had to broach the awkward subject of the shipping agent.

'Madame, I know that some agreement was made between your people and a shipping agent to take Pierre from Rouen to London. Presumably, money changed hands also. Do you have the name of that agent?'

Her face turned even darker.

'Indeed, it was a shipping agent who worked out of Rouen. Pierre and I had arrived in the town on the back of a horse and cart. We stayed in a poor hotel while I considered what I should do next. After the first day, I noticed the British ship the *Spirit of Rochester*, docked on the jetty. I found out who its shipping agent was and paid him for Pierre to be taken on board and brought to London. This was unofficial you understand, no paperwork, no passports – he would just be shown where to hide on the ship then emerge at the port of London free from danger. The agent's name was Michael Bernard. It seemed a reputable shipping firm, with offices in London. I then left Pierre and travelled by train overland to Brussels where I met the French Ambassador. He then made the arrangements for me to travel to Cassel in Germany, via Cologne, to re-join Louis Napoleon. I assumed that everything was fine with Pierre and that he was safe, so I travelled to Germany in good heart – happy to serve my Emperor.'

'Why did you not want to join Empress Eugenie in England? That way you could have escorted Pierre and seen that he was safe?'

She grimaced. 'I know I did the wrong thing now but – let me put it this way – myself and Eugenie do not always see eye to eye. She is jealous of my friendship with Louis – my loyalty was to him, not her.' I nodded. There was a ring of truth about that.

'So, I was taken to the chateau in Cassel, where he was held captive, and I soon settled into the routine. Louis was grateful to see me and impressed by my loyalty. All was well, or as well as anything can be when you have lost your liberty. Then I got a message from London that Pierre had not arrived. I was mortified by this, but what could I do? It was too late; we were stuck in Prussia under house arrest. It was only after we had been released from Cassel and travelled to England in March this year that I was able to start searching for my boy.'

She was clearly distressed but continued, 'Obviously, when Pierre didn't arrive in London my people contacted the shipping agents, asking what was going on. They denied all knowledge of the transaction, said they had never heard of Michael Bernard, and that he was a swindler who purported to be from their company. We gave them a description of the agent, but they said that it did not match with anyone who worked for them.'

We both looked glumly at each other.

'My only clue was this report of a boy being rowed ashore at Gravesend. Could it be my Pierre? That is why I have come here.'

We walked on, in an easterly direction towards the fort, in silence. One part of me felt an awkwardness at the silence yet another part rather liked the peaceful joy of walking beside a beautiful lady along the riverside in the glorious summer weather. We were now on the section of promenade overlooked by the fort. She broke the silence.

'Tell me something of yourself William, I have not even asked if you are married with children?'

'No, I am still a bachelor – I make a living out of journalism and hunting down missing people. I fought in Crimea – where I met Charles Gordon. Beyond that there is not much to tell.'

She seemed to find this of interest and smiled. I decided to probe a little, as for the first time since we met she seemed relaxed.

'And what of yourself Marie, your background?'

She tensed, the softness in her face momentarily hardened.

'I think it is as well we keep things on a business footing Mr Reeves. I do not have time for small talk.' At that she quickened her pace and I quickly realised where I stood in our relationship.

'Pardon me, madame, for being forward. Could we then talk some more about the arrangement entered into to get Pierre out of Paris and into England?'

She looked even more vexed by this question.

'William, I have told you everything I know. When Pierre left Rouen, the Emperor and half his court were already in prison in Prussia. I travelled by train to Cassel to join him. We were then stuck there all winter, from September through to this March. That is why I speak good English. As I had little to do, I studied it every day. Not that you have commented on it.'

I could see she was not going to let me off the hook this time.

She continued in her cool, offhand tone, 'Now if you would excuse me, I would prefer to walk back to the Clarendon on my own.' I inwardly flinched at this but tried to keep the calm atmosphere going.

'Of course, mademoiselle, I understand. Shall we meet again tomorrow?'

'Of course, same time, and I expect some progress by then.' At this she opened her parasol to protect her face from the warm sun and walked off in the direction of the hotel alone.

EIGHT

The Mud Larkers

I STOOD FOR A MOMENT, a little unsure as to how to proceed. My thoughts were soon disturbed by a voice on the fort parapet behind me. It was Gordon, silhouetted against the bright afternoon sun.

'Stay there a moment Reeves, I'd like a word with you.' Gordon quickly made haste down the grassy bank of the fort then across the short stretch of cobbles to where I was standing. 'So, Reeves, I see your charm has not yet worked on the mademoiselle? I would be careful there if I were you.' I must have looked suitably chastened.

'I am just trying to get some sort of angle on this. She is telling me so much, but I think not everything. It is all very frustrating.' Gordon looked almost fatherly at this point. 'You have to keep going.' He smiled at me and took in the view. 'Look, let us go down by the boats and see if the mud larks are working today.'

We strode out along the pathway back towards the town pier. Finally, I realised what he was referring to. Alongside the pier I could see some grubby-looking boys on the foreshore, poking about in the dirty Thames water. 'I think we are in luck Reeves. One of the boys who was in my school, an orphan, is over there. Let us see if we can get his attention.'

Gordon shouted to the boy. 'Fred, come over here.' The boy looked over, and seeing it was Gordon, clambered up the bank from the foreshore to where we were standing. Gordon obviously knew the boy.

'Now Fred, this gentleman here is William Reeves, a friend of mine, who has a few questions for you.' The boy looked underfed and sullen but swarthy – probably due to spending so much time outside; he also smelt badly of the river.

'What's in it for me, sir?' he said begrudgingly. Gordon was not happy at this. 'I think Fred you should be grateful for the help I have given you in the past. Getting you a warm bed in winter and food for your belly. Nevertheless, I'll give you a florin for any information you can give us.'

The boy thought for a moment then said, 'Half a crown would be better.' Gordon sighed. 'Very well. Go ahead Reeves.' I looked squarely at the boy.

'Now Fred, I appreciate the questions I'm going to ask are sensitive but if you could help it might save another boy's life. Alright?' Fred grunted. 'Very well, now the rumour is that by the foreshore, behind the King's Arms, there is a spot where sailors and customers of the pub have been known to touch boys, is that true?'

Gordon was clearly uncomfortable, but Fred did not bat an eyelid.

'They'se do more than touching, sir, I've seen all sorts going on. I was told there was easy money to be made so I went there, and a man paid me a shilling to feel me privates. I thought that was alright but when I went back the next time, they wanted a lot more – so I told them dirty bastards where to go.'

Gordon looked displeased. There was an awkward silence, which Fred finally filled.

'I'm sorry sir for allowing it to happen, I know God will be displeased by the way I was, but I weren't as bad as some of the boys. I couldn't repeat what was done to them.' Gordon was now apoplectic with anger.

'I don't know if I want to hear any more of this ungodly talk.'

I felt his embarrassment but needed this information so pressed the lad further. 'Now Fred, these nasty men; were they all customers of the King's Arms?'

'I think so sir. Thing is there's an alleyway that goes from the backroom of the pub down to the water's edge – so they can slip out, pretend they are going to the latrines and instead go around the back to where the boys are waiting.'

Gordon was still red-faced. 'This is so disgusting,' he said through clenched teeth.

I ignored him and continued. 'Do you know if one of these men was a Captain Lynch from the *Spirit of Rochester*?'

The boy thought but not for long. 'I have no idea sir who the men are, some are sailors, some quite respectable-looking, but I don't know no names.'

I thought this was an honest answer so decided enough was enough for now.

'Thanks Fred, you have been most useful. One more question though, if this is going on, and you must know it's illegal, why aren't the Gravesend constabulary getting involved?'

Fred shrugged his shoulders. 'Don't know sir, though nobody can see round the back of the pub from the street – part of the alleyway gets blocked at high tide, so people think you can't get through. You can't see what's going on from the river either because of the building overhanging the alley.'

I got another shilling out of my pocket. 'Thanks for being so honest with us.'

Gordon had clearly been discomforted but had remained composed.

'Yes, thank you Fred, you can get back to your work now.'

The boy smiled. 'No way, I'm going to treat myself to some fish and chips now I've got me shillings.' At that he scampered off in the direction of the town.

I stood there in silence with Gordon, who was clearly still upset by the discussion. He spoke first.

'So, what was the point of that? I do not want to hear about such disgusting activity. I've a good mind to go into the King's Arms with a bucket of spirits and burn the place down.'

I could feel his pain.

'I am sorry for having to do that but to solve this case I may need to put the frighteners on Lynch. If he felt that he was being investigated for lewd behaviour with children, then he might crack.'

Gordon had now calmed down.

'I know what you're trying to do Reeves, but the boy clearly has no idea who the perpetrators were. I do not think we have even got enough to get the constabulary involved yet. You can be sure that the pub will have a look-out system and if a man in uniform approaches they will have the rear alleyway cleared of people in seconds.' I nodded, he continued.

'This whole business makes me sick. I am constantly depressed by the ungodly behaviour of these people: they are the devil's work. But I know we have work to do to bring light into this darkness.'

We both stood in silence for a while. I could see two Thames barges with their blood-red sails stretched against the breeze moving downstream in the sunshine. So much beauty amongst this ugliness. Gordon finally turned to me.

'Reeves, let us give this more thought. I have work to do.' He turned away, then as a passing shot said, 'By the way, have you had any response to your posters? I've seen them all around town.'

'No, nothing at all yet.'

He sighed then made his way back to the fort. I went my own way, along the promenade in the opposite direction.

I walked for a long while along the river, thinking things through. I knew I owed it to Marie and Gordon to crack this case, but no strong leads had presented themselves yet. I finally made my way back to the Eagle, much depressed by what I had heard.

NINE

Lynch

BACK IN MY ROOM I still had no sense of rest or relief, so I placed my chair by the window from where I could see one of my posters, displayed on a tree in West Street, not far from the King's Arms. I sat there for an exceedingly long time. I noted that though many people looked at the picture of the lost boy, they were mostly older, respectable citizens of the town, people unlikely to have had any involvement in Pierre's disappearance. Finally, though, a more interesting character stopped, and read the poster diligently. On reading it he looked around furtively, then read it again before walking off. At last – here was a man who might have seen this boy before! What was also pleasing was that the man was dark-skinned, probably a lascar seaman from east Africa. If so, perhaps he might have been on the *Spirit* when the boy was on board? My thoughts raced away. Do I run down and grab him? Plead with him to get the truth? Or play it slowly? Just forcing him to tell me all would probably go nowhere; he could simply deny all knowledge. So, I decided to take my time. Finally, after much rumination I went down to the bar of the Eagle to see if I could prise some information from the innkeeper, Samuel.

Luckily, the bar was not too crowded tonight, so after ordering my usual whiskey and water, I was able to converse with Sam. I knew from experience that to glean information from him, you had to play to his prejudices and never ask a straight question.

My opener was, 'I was looking out of my window just before I came down, Sam. I saw a lascar in the street, off one of the boats. Don't understand why we are employing foreigners when good British men have no work.'

He rose to the bait immediately.

'Well, that is the state this country is in – it would rather give work to foreigners than our own people. Truth is, the lascars are cheap, pay them pennies and they are happy. It is the boat captains that are the worst offenders. I expect the lascar was off the *Spirit of Rochester*, their captain, Lynch, is a right tight arse – but don't go repeating that in company.'

'Is the *Spirit of Rochester* in Gravesend then?'

He looked at me and smiled knowingly. 'Of course it is, you can see it from our window here.'

I leapt up from my bar stool and in a few paces was staring out of the window. There it was, bold as brass. I returned to the bar to quickly finish my whiskey and probe Sam further. 'How long has it been in port?'

'Not long, came up early evening on the tide. I expect by now the crew and Lynch are in the King's Arms. They never come in here, which is a blessing, believe me.'

I made ready to quickly leave. Sam looked quizzically at me. 'You're not thinking of going to the King's Arms, are you? You want to be careful there. Lynch can be a tricky customer.'

I smiled at Sam. 'I can be pretty tricky myself.'

I walked out into West Street and quickly made the 100 yards to the door of the King's Arms. I had no real plan of action but needed to take this chance of seeing Lynch in person. The pub was obviously older and rougher than the Eagle. There was sawdust on the floor and many men, obviously seamen, were getting drunk very quickly. I did not let this deter me and went straight over to the barman and ordered a whiskey. The barman was a tough-looking fellow with a heavily lined face and purple nose, caused no doubt by too many years of heavy drinking. He looked at me without great emotion but cautiously. 'You're not a regular in here are you sir? I will not be serving gentlemen tonight as I have got a boat in. You best be on your way.'

I looked back at him slightly surprised by this turn of events.

'I assumed my money was as good as any seaman, but in any case, I have not come here for your whiskey. I've come to see Captain John Lynch of the *Spirit of Rochester*.' I paused to await his response, perhaps I am imagining it, but the inn seemed suddenly quieter. The barman looked unhappy at this suggestion.

'I don't think Mr Lynch is taking visitors. Now be on your way.' I looked back at him and held my ground – I also noted the stairs further into the inn, which presumably led to a room upstairs. I could hear noise from above, from somewhere near the top of the staircase, so I quickly set off across the sawdust floor and taking two steps at a time, walked up those stairs to the next floor. At the top, there was a lobby, leading off this was an unguarded door. I opened it. I was immediately assailed by the noise and smells of many seamen drinking together. Before me I could see what I assume were the senior crew of the *Spirit* sitting alongside a long table that stretched most of the length of the room. In the centre of it was a tough, grey-haired man, in full sea captain's uniform, with a face that looked as if it has been carved out of granite. Even his grey hair was not the grey of old age, more the grey of wrought ironwork. He stared at me and spat out the words, 'Who are you? This is a private function, get out.'

I could see his henchmen making ready to see me off in good style, so I got my piece in first.

'Captain John Lynch I assume.'

He stared back impassively, this was his kingdom and he was the undisputed king. I continued, 'I'd like to ask you about the disappearance of a French national, Pierre Le Beau, who I believe you brought from Rouen as a stowaway, last September?'

No sooner had the word left my mouth than two heavies had grabbed my arms and prepared to chuck me out. Lynch looked on with disdain and stated loudly,

'I don't know anything about that. Never heard of this Pierre, never seen him, I have already had the Excise people going on about this. I do not know who you are, but you're not welcome. Now sling your hook, or I'll give you a beating you won't forget.'

I had nothing more to say, I knew this had been a futile gesture but wanted to see this Lynch, face to face.

'Alright, I'm going, get your hands off me.' They loosened their grip and I departed down the stairs with eyes following my every move. I then headed out towards the main pub door to the street. I was just about to exit when I saw the lascar I had seen looking at the poster, sitting quietly in the corner. I made a mental note of this.

Outside the inn it was a glorious warm evening and the sunlight was dazzling after the darkness of the pub's interior. On this beautiful night, local couples were walking down the street, arm in arm, promenading and enjoying the weather, completely oblivious to what was happening inside and worse, at the back of that inn. I thought of the earlier conversations with Gordon and the boy Fred. It seemed incredible that just a few yards from the civility of the street, in this relatively prosperous riverside town, such behaviour could go unchallenged. However, I could also see how the constabulary would struggle to police the goings-on at the back, as the pub was part of a terrace and the riverside alley could not be seen from the street.

I walked back to the Eagle a little frustrated by my lack of progress but pleased that I had finally met in person the devil himself. Also, the lascar was a possible lead; his facial expression when looking at the poster convinced me that my gut instinct was correct. He had seen the boy on board the boat – he knew that something was wrong. It was a small lead, but better than nothing.

I slept a little more soundly that night, I knew that somehow, some way, I could crack this problem and find the boy.

TEN

The Brewery Boys

I WOKE EARLY WITH THE sound of the dray horses' hoofs clattering down the cobbled street. The drayman always started off early. They were impeccably dressed for working men, with dark green uniforms finished off with black bowler hats. Their presence reminded me I had yet to interview John Bennett, the shipping company agent. That would be my first task today. After dressing and breakfast, I walked the few yards down to the brewery yard and looked in. All around were dray horses and carts laden with beer kegs. At the back of the yard was what looked like a cooper's workshop, where damaged wooden kegs could be made and repaired. Running alongside the yard were a set of iron stairs leading onto a gantry at first floor level, and along this were what looked like offices. Nobody stopped me, so I simply walked up the staircase, my feet clanking on the metalwork at my feet. Then along the gantry. Still no one asked my business. I must presumably look respectable. The offices all seemed to be connected to the brewery in some way, apart from the last one I came to. Though small, it would be the only office with a window looking out onto the Thames. On its door in small print were the words 'John Bennett – Shipping agent'. I knocked on the door.

'Come in, it's open.'

Sitting on a stool by a high slanted table, writing in a heavy ledger, was the small man that I had seen from a distance every morning. I thrust out my hand.

'Mr Bennett, I presume.'

He stuttered slightly, clearly discomforted by my appearance.

'Yes, and what is your business, sir?'

'My name is William Reeves and I'm looking into the disappearance of a French national, Pierre Le Beau – who I understand was brought into Gravesend by your company on September 17th last year.'

His face registered displeasure at this, like a man who has sucked an under-ripe lemon.

'I have already spoken to the Excise, and the constabulary, about this issue. My company knows nothing of this person. Now I would bid you good day.' He got up from his stool and deliberately opened the door to usher me out.

'I'm sorry Mr Bennett then for wasting your time. You must appreciate that in cases of missing persons, especially when the person is a child, things are sensitive, and I must explore all avenues.' He seemed to relax slightly at this point and spoke in a more measured tone.

'I fully understand, and if I could be of help in this matter, I certainly would.'

I smiled. 'Thank you, if anything comes to mind, here is my card, I am staying at the Eagle. Oh, and here is a poster showing Pierre.'

I slowly eased the poster from my coat pocket and unfolding it, handed it to Bennett. 'As you can see, he is only young, and his mother is traumatised by his loss.'

Bennett nodded. 'I quite understand Mr Reeves but I'm a busy man and have much to attend to.'

I also nodded. 'Of course, you must be. I see one of your ships, the *Spirit of Rochester*, is in port now. I'm sure there's plenty of paperwork to be catching up on.'

'Yes, indeed, I shall be busy.' I shook his hand and then made to leave. I stopped just before closing the door and turned back to him. 'I am an old military man Mr Bennett. Your limp, did you get it in service in the Crimea by any chance?'

He looked slightly abashed.

'No, it was from falling off a horse, I was a trainee jockey and had a bad fall, almost lost the leg.'

I tried to look concerned. 'Horses, they can be difficult beasts. Do you still ride?' He nodded. 'Yes, I live on the outskirts of the town so ride in every day.'

I reached out and shook his hand. 'Good for you, never let a setback stop you from doing what you want to do, that's what I say.'

At that I departed and walked back along the gantry. I noted that at the very back of the yard were stables, one housing the massive, magnificent drays, the other workaday horses suitable for riding to and from work. I went down the stairs and left the brewery.

For some reason I decided to go for a long walk to try and get my thoughts together. I had an hour or so to kill until I met Marie again, so I wandered the streets of Gravesend aimlessly. Little did I know that at Chislehurst, events were already starting to unfold.

ELEVEN

Chislehurst

THE FRENCH COURT OF LOUIS Napoleon had moved into Camden Place in Chislehurst, ten miles out from London, in October 1870.

Initially it was the home of Napoleon's Empress, Eugenie, and her entourage. Then the following March, Napoleon himself had been released from imprisonment in Germany and was able to join her. He brought with him his own people who had shared his imprisonment over winter. So, by the summer of 1871 the Emperor in exile and his wife were living in a large detached mansion in Kent, with a large number of staff with little to do.

Camden Place was a grand affair – with its own spacious grounds and gated driveway framed by ancient elm trees. However, Napoleon was only there because of his wealth and friendship with Queen Victoria – Louis now had only minor importance in French life, and in international politics wielded no power, and had little hope of ever again being Emperor. So, the French court was impotent and pointless, full of too many people trying to justify their existence.

As Marie had not arrived until March, and was forever out of favour with Eugenie, she had lost her position as her Lady-in-Waiting and was now being kept away from helping the Emperor; this role being given to a nurse, as Louis was often ill with his bladder and gallstone problems.

One of the chief taskmasters of this toxic atmosphere was the head of household, Matthew Toulouse – who had Napoleon's ear. Today, as per usual, he had woken early and with great ceremony walked the rooms of the mansion checking that all was in order and impeccably clean. Camden Place was an old house, recently refurbished and in its style and grandeur, similar to the fine chateaus of his homeland. Toulouse inspected the main hallway and had already noted something that needed addressing. He pointed this out to Elizabeth Bouchard, the chief housekeeper, who had just emerged from the card room.

'*Bonjour,* Mademoiselle Bouchard. I note that the flowers look a little tired. Can you explain that?'

Bouchard looked back at him, there was no love lost between them.

'I'm sorry, but flower arranging is done by Marie-Anne. That is her domain.'

Toulouse was having none of this. 'As you know Marie, along with Antonia, has gone away for a few days' rest and relaxation.'

Bouchard scoffed. 'Rest and relaxation? She has done nothing since she came here! Why does she need rest?' Toulouse disregarded her comment and continued.

'If you could just get some fresh flowers. That will be all.'

Bouchard slipped away, clearly displeased at this telling off.

Just then there was a knock on the front door. Toulouse, still in a foul humour, walked over to open it. Standing there before him was Monsieur Jerome, head of security.

'Here is a letter for the Emperor. It was left at the gatehouse by somebody during the night. We think it may have been dropped there by a man on horseback.'

He handed over a bulky envelope. Toulouse looked at it carefully.

'Very well, leave this to me. That will be all.'

At this, Jerome departed, and the front door was shut. Toulouse gingerly opened the letter and carefully read its contents. Then, without hesitation, he set off up the grand staircase to the first-floor bedroom where Napoleon slept.

TWELVE

Things Get Darker

I HAD WALKED FOR OVER an hour and was now minded getting back to the Eagle to prepare for my afternoon visit to see Marie. It was getting close to three o'clock and I always liked to be ready early for those meetings. Just as I came within sight of the Eagle, I could see Gordon standing outside, presumably waiting to see me. It was strange to see him outside of the fort, in his Royal Engineers' uniform. He looked like a fish out of water. One thing I noted immediately was how well known and popular he was, virtually everyone bade him good day and other words of respect. I walked up to him and opened the conversation.

'Are you looking for me?' He sighed and gently nudged me to the side of the road, out of earshot of passers-by. As usual, he came straight to the point: 'Reeves, I'm afraid I have some bad news. Things are getting serious. One of Napoleon's security staff at Camden Place at Chislehurst has telegraphed today with information. It appears that this morning a letter was received – it had been left at the gatehouse so there is no postmark to go on. It was addressed to Napoleon himself.'

'And what were the contents of the letter?'

'Unfortunately, the envelope contained a message stating that they had the boy, Pierre, and that he was imprisoned at an unspecified location. They would release him if a fee of ten thousand guineas, in gold, was forthcoming. There is no further information on likely drop-off points, or how this exchange is to happen. There was also a lock of Pierre's hair, which apparently matches their memory of him. It says that should attempts be made to rescue him, he will be killed. The letter finishes by stating that further contact will be made shortly to agree terms of the exchange.'

I looked back at Gordon; things were clearly getting serious. 'So, what are we to do about that?'

'No idea Reeves, but I think your first duty is to update Marie-Anne on this development.'

'Very well, I'm due to meet her at three o'clock today so will do so then.' Gordon nodded assent. 'Good, but tread carefully. This news will come as a terrible shock to her. I'll leave it in your hands.' Gordon then made to walk off back to the fort but within a few paces was stopped by another well-wisher. A man who appeared to be a worker from the brewery.

'Good afternoon, sir. Sorry for interrupting your walk, but I just thought I would let you know that I am back at the brewery – working as the night watchman. If all goes well I will be back on the drays in a few months.'

Gordon smiled. 'That is exceptionally good news.'

The man smiled broadly. 'Thank you sir, sorry to disturb you.'

At that he bowed to Gordon and to myself and walked back into the brewery.

Gordon filled me in with the detail once he was out of earshot.

'That man is Jessie Armitage. Son died in awful circumstances, so he reached for the bottle. Almost lost his job in the brewery but he seems on the mend now.' He paused a second. 'I'll get back to the fort.'

I nodded and he swiftly strode off.

It was now almost three o'clock, so without delay I walked over to the Clarendon. I had some bad news to impart so wanted to reach Marie before she got to the restaurant.

At the hotel lobby I waited around until I saw Marie and Antonia making their way down the staircase en route to the restaurant. I spoke immediately.

'Can I take you for a walk alone, Marie? I have some news.' Marie looked slightly perturbed but agreed without hesitation and sent Antonia away. We walked out into the street and I led her towards the riverside green where benches faced onto the water. She looked at me quizzically as we walked but said nothing.

Having sat down on a bench, she swivelled to look at me full on.

'What is it William. Why are we here?'

I gathered my strength.

'Marie, I have to tell you this. Lieutenant-Colonel Gordon received a telegram from the Emperor at Chislehurst this morning. It appears that a letter containing a ransom demand for ten thousand guineas in gold was received overnight. That would be the price of them releasing Pierre.

That is all the gist of it. They also included a lock of your boy's hair.' Marie gasped and was clearly close to tears. I continued.

'The letter ends by stating that they will give further information as to the place and time for the exchange of gold, or Pierre, later. The letter writer also threatens to kill Pierre immediately, if the police get involved.'

Marie looked mortified, awfully close to tears. I wished that I had broken the news more gently but what could I say that would bring any comfort? In my heart I just wanted to put my arms around Marie and hug her and tell her it would be alright. She finally found some words.

'So, what can we do? I have no money. Nobody cares enough to find ten thousand guineas. What can we do?' Her eyes pleaded with me. I tried my best to seem organised.

'This is clearly very upsetting but at least we now know that Pierre is probably alive, albeit hidden somewhere. At least this gives us a chance of finding him, of somehow releasing him.'

She just seemed shocked beyond words and just sat there. The wind blew in off the river, her face looked broken; she was utterly disconsolate. 'What can we do William, what can we do?'

'Let me speak to Gordon about this to see if he has any further ideas. But please do not upset yourself. We will find your son and he will come back to you safe and sound, I promise this.'

At this she seemed to calm down a little. She reached out and gently held my hand by her fingertips.

'Thank you, William, without you I would be totally lost.'

I reached down gently and softly kissed her hand.

'Mademoiselle.'

I took her arm and gently led her back to the hotel. We parted company at the lobby. She was going back to her room to lie down. I desperately wanted to ease her distress but had no idea how. I bade goodbye.

There was no alternative other than to see Gordon again and ask what his thoughts were on this crisis.

Within minutes I was back at the fort, and luckily was able to speak to him immediately. Sadly, our conversation yielded little more. He believed that Napoleon's court, though probably wealthy, would not wish to be seen to be too involved. It would also be very awkward if news of this reached Queen Victoria. Pierre after all was in any case a 'bastard' and not the legitimate son of the Emperor. Napoleon already had a legitimate son, also called Louis, of similar age to Pierre who was living at Camden Place.

We both sat there in Gordon's spartan office, trawling our brains for any sort of lead as to the whereabouts of the boy. I felt that the only way forward was to go back to the initial deal between the shipping agent and Marie, to bring Pierre to England. That brought the conversation back to John Bennett. Gordon knew something of the man's business. It appeared that Bennett had got his office on the brewery site when the paddle steamer pleasure boats started taking daytrippers to Margate and Clacton. He had since diversified into flint and chalk shipping, taking these commodities from northern France and the chalk pits around Gravesend. From here they were shipped up north, with his biggest market being the potteries, via the port of Liverpool. So, Bennett probably knew Rouen well, and could have been implicated in organising the abduction. However, we had no proof. No real leads as to where Pierre was being hidden, or even if he was still alive.

Our conversation went on like this for the best part of an hour. Finally, I thanked Gordon for his help and left the fort. I was by now feeling even more downhearted as I walked back to the Eagle. This was a problem that was beating me hands down. I had received little response from the posters, nobody knew anything of Pierre's whereabouts, and it was almost impossible to pay the ransom demanded. But then I had a lucky break. As I passed the Three Daws I noticed to my left, walking up the high street opposite, the lascar I had seen looking at the poster. I decided to follow him. He seemed unaware of my presence as he walked up the high street before disappearing into the market building behind the courthouse. I followed him into the market and was soon enveloped in the cacophony of noise and colour, as the costermongers bid to outshout each other. The market was a buyer's dream, with stalls selling everything you could dream of.

I kept the lascar in my sight and could see him buying some vegetables and fruit from one of the costermongers and putting them into a basket. I waited until he retraced his steps and left the market past the courthouse in the high street. I quickened my pace and got in front of him. Then stopped dead, and staring him straight in the eye, confronted him.

'Excuse me, let me introduce myself, I am William Reeves. Can I speak with you on a matter of some importance?' At this I could see the colour draining from his face. I pressed him further.

'Do you speak English?'

He replied in stilted but perfectly understandable English.

'Yes, sir, certainly sir.'

I responded, 'I am a private detective, and I'm looking for a lost boy. I believe he may have been picked up on your ship, the *Spirit of Rochester*, in France. Do you know anything of this?'

He was clearly scared.

'Yes, sir, I am a seaman from that ship. Sir, I am just buying provisions. I do not know what you are talking about. I am sorry, I cannot help you.'

I could see from his expression that he had a lowly position on the boat and was likely to be subservient in manner to any well-dressed white man. I continued.

'Look, I know you know more than you're telling me. I saw you spending a long time looking at the poster of the lost boy, pinned on the tree in West Street. You recognised the boy in the picture, didn't you?'

He became even more flustered at this.

'No sir, I have never seen this boy.' His awkwardness betrayed him, so I continued to pursue him.

'The boy Pierre, he got on the boat at Rouen didn't he – as a stowaway but you knew he was there on board, didn't you?'

His face was now ashen. 'I am sorry sir, I know nothing.'

I was not letting him get away.

'Where are you from and what is your name?'

He stumbled over his words but replied, 'I am Asif Khan, and my home is in Zanzibar.' I smiled encouragingly.

'Now Asif, I'm sure you're a good man but you also have a secret – you have seen this boy before and if you don't tell me what you know I am going to stab myself with this knife.' I pulled a letter opener from my coat pocket. 'And I will say that you knifed me in a bungled robbery. You know what the Gravesend constabulary will do to you then?'

He clearly believed all this. 'No, sir.'

I pressed home my advantage.

'Well you would probably stand trial in the building behind you, and if you were lucky you would end up in one of Her Majesty's prisons. If you were unlucky you would get the noose. You would certainly never see Zanzibar again.' He stood looking at me in silence, grabbing his basket of fruit ever closer to his chest. He looked around surreptitiously – then jerked his head indicating I should follow him.

Between the shops, opposite the courthouse, was an alleyway just wide enough for one man to pass through. He walked into it with me behind him, all the time looking over his shoulder to see if anyone was looking at us. There were people in the street, but none was taking any notice, and within seconds we were out of eye and earshot of the busy street. Inside the alleyway he seemed to relax.

'If I tell you what I know, you must please never say I said it, otherwise I will be dead.'

I nodded.

'This boy, Pierre you say his name is, came on board at night in Rouen. He was locked in the hold until we had reached Gravesend. Then just before we docked, he was put on a rowing boat and taken ashore. That was before we got to the Customs check. That is all I know. I never spoke to him. Never had anything to do with it. Now, can I go, please sir?'

At last!

'Yes, you can go now.' He looked back at me, clearly scared witless.

'Please, do not tell anyone what I have said. Captain Lynch would flail me alive if he knew.'

I felt slightly sorry for him.

'Of course, we never had this meeting, you told me nothing. Now, you had best get back to the boat with your fruit.'

At that he scampered off, out of the alley down the high street. I knew what I had done was unethical but sometimes desperate times needed desperate action. I walked back to the Eagle with a spring in my step, feeling that some progress was now being made.

THIRTEEN

Another Visitor

As I ARRIVED AT THE Eagle, I was greeted by Jack Carter. He was leaning on a polished wooden walking stick and puffing away vigorously on his pipe. He smelt of damp clothes and tobacco.

'Mr Reeves, can I have a word please?'

I smiled, surprised by this turn of events. 'Of course. Would you like somewhere more private?'

He nodded in agreement.'

' Let us go up to my room then.'

I led him through the reception area up the stairs and into my modest bedroom on the first floor. I could see climbing stairs was not really his forte but clearly he had some information to impart. We sat down.

'So, Jack, to what do I owe this pleasant surprise?'

He took out his pipe and gently tapped its contents into an ashtray on the small, round table in the room.

'Well, the truth is William, if I might call you by your first name? It appears that I might have been leading you up the garden path, so to speak, about the sighting of the rowing boat leaving the *Spirit of Rochester*.' He looked a little awkward at this point.

'Go on.'

'Well after you had visited my house I went back over my records for the 17th September 1870 and I realised that I had entered the sighting of the rowing boat under completely the wrong date. I was a month out you see, so by a process of deduction that means I was noting down a rowing boat coming ashore on the 17th October. Now that would point to the boat being the schooner *Burgundy* and not the *Spirit...*' He stopped talking to let the words sink in. I feigned shock and replied.

'Well, that is a great shame, I have been following enquires based on the fact that it was the *Spirit* that the rowing boat came from. This rather ruins my whole case.'

He nodded.

'I'm obviously deeply sorry to have led you astray like this; normally I'm totally accurate on matters of recording detail. I really don't know how this could have occurred.'

I decided to play along with his fairy tale and feigned grievous disappointment.

'This puts me back to square one, I am really shocked that this could happen. Is there no chance you might be mistaken?'

He sighed.

'No, I'm terribly sorry for leading you in the wrong direction. Now if you'll forgive me I'll be on my way.'

I put out my hand and shook his.

'Well, thank you for being so honest with me. I will have to consider what further enquiries can be made in the light of this news.' We shook hands; he turned and left my room. I closed the door then moved to the window.

Some twenty seconds later he emerged onto the street below me. I stood at an angle to the window to remain unseen. He then slowly walked off down West Street – I kept looking until he passed the King's Arms. I then noticed a chink of light from one of the first-floor windows of the inn. A face, perhaps John Lynch himself, was peering through the lace curtains – looking down. Without breaking stride Carter turned to look up at the figure, nodded, then carried on down the street. The lace curtain fell back into place, and the face at the first-floor window was gone. It was as I thought: Carter was doing Lynch a favour and trying to throw me off the scent.

I sat down in the room to compose my thoughts. So, Lynch knew I was on his track and was making sure I got no further. Clearly he was a dangerous man, he had probably threatened to burn down Carter's house if he did not tell me a pack of lies. Perhaps I was next, a knife in the back down some quiet alley. Just another murder in this rough sailors' town? I had to keep going now I knew for sure the boy had come to Gravesend, and might be still here, in the town, or nearby, imprisoned.

FOURTEEN

The Town
and Country

My head was reeling, so I decided to go for a long walk. It was a nice enough day though it seemed to be growing more humid. I left the Eagle and strode along the high street up to the station. There, I turned left and walked in an easterly direction. This brought me to the north end of Wellington Street, which I then walked up. It was odd how so many streets were now being named after battles of the Napoleonic Wars, and British military heroes. Even worse was the recent naming of streets after battles in the Crimea war – typical examples being Alma and Sevastopol. If only the road builders had actually experienced the horror of war they might have chosen other names! It also served as a reminder to me that tomorrow, the 18th June, was Waterloo Day, and sixteen years to the day when I was wounded at the siege of Sevastopol in the Crimea.

At the top of Wellington Street, I reached Windmill Hill and from there I could look over the open countryside towards the river. This was free draining chalkland, dry and sun-baked in summer and mud free in the winter. The exact opposite to the marshlands and mudflats that separated it from the river. I noted a well-used path through the grassland and walked along it in a north-easterly direction towards the Thames, which meandered towards the estuary, a mile or two beyond Gravesend.

As I walked, the thoughts and meetings over the last few days filled my head. What Jack Carter said about getting the dates of the sighting wrong was clearly a deliberate lie, and an attempt to throw me off the scent. The truth was that Pierre had been on the *Spirit* and had been brought ashore, probably somewhere to the east of the town. At least my conversation with Asif had confirmed this, but if still alive, where was the boy now?

I sat down on a sturdy timber bench and looked at the panorama before me. My feelings were that Pierre was likely to be held captive somewhere near to the riverside port area of the town. I had come to this conclusion quickly. The facts were that Gravesend was now mostly a settled town with a stable population – any newcomers or unusual comings and goings would be noted and perhaps reported to the constabulary. Outside the town were the Thames marshes, which stretched down to the estuary. The people who lived here were even more embedded in their landscape. They were a long-standing and resolute community of mostly graziers, who had lived on the marshes forever. In fact, 'outsiders' often struggled to adapt to life on the marshes and suffered terribly from the ague or marsh fever, which was deadly in many cases.

No, if the boy were being held around here it would be in the West Street area of the riverside, where sailors from far away countries were a normal occurrence, and there was a constant movement of people coming to and leaving the port.

I gazed at the horizon and noted the beauty of the boats on the river, almost invisible at this distance, but still giving the scene a serene charm on this warm exquisite night.

As I sat on the bench, a young couple passed deep in conversation, and holding each other close. This was clearly a place for courting couples. How I would have loved to take Marie here, and be that close to her! I quickly put the idea out of my mind, but not without difficulty! Though I could hardly admit it to myself, I was very attracted to the French Emperor's woman.

I moved on. At the bottom of the open down land, I crossed over the Rochester road and walked on past some new housing. I was now in a place called Denton. I then followed a lane which took me over the railway lines and beyond them, a noticeably quiet canal. Another 200 yards and I had reached the Thames foreshore. Here was the little community of Denton. It had a pub, the Ship and Lobster, overlooking the river, and a shipbreakers' yard. The sign above the yard stated 'Tibbalds shipbreakers and timber suppliers'. I wondered if it would be possible to get inside the site, but the yard had a sturdy gate and perimeter wall, so I explored no further. However, I noted the smell of tar in the breeze, presumably coming off the rotting boats being dismembered for scrap. There was not much else to see, so I headed west along the foreshore towards Gravesend. On my way I passed the canal basin and the fort and arrived back at my hotel before sunset.

As it was too early for bed I stayed in the bar for a while, refreshing myself with a pint of porter – I was too thirsty for my usual whiskey. I saw that the barman Sam was not too busy so decide to engage him in conversation. We talked about not very much for a while but then I remembered it was Waterloo Day tomorrow, so questioned him on what happened in the town on that day. His face was in equal measures excited and angry.

'Waterloo Day! It should be banned if you ask me. The town goes a bit mad. Sometimes the sailors roll barrels of flaming tar down the high street. Have you ever heard of anything so stupid? I'm only glad I don't have a pub on that street.'

'That sounds interesting. What boats would the sailors be coming from?'

'Usual suspects. Lynch will be there, with his men from the *Spirit*. Likes to show them who is boss. To be honest a gentleman like yourself might want to avoid the whole thing.'

I nodded in affirmation, delighted in receiving this information. This could be another chance to see Lynch close up, an opportunity that Marie might wish to share with me.

I bade Sam goodnight and went to bed.

That night I slept badly. Too much was rattling through my brain and the night was hot and sticky. I consoled myself with the thought that Waterloo Day could be the breakthrough we needed.

FIFTEEN

Back to Marie-Anne

I RETURNED TO THE CLARENDON at 3 p.m. exactly and
entered the restaurant. There was Marie with her maid,
sipping from china cups as if they did not have a care in the
world. I was ushered to my seat while Antonia poured coffee
and arranged biscuits on a plate. Marie was back to her old
self-contained self. The pain of yesterday's news seemed to
have gone, and she was as elegant and well-spoken as always.

'So, have we any further information, William?'

'Yes, I intercepted a crewman from the *Spirit*, a lascar
called Asif.'

She looked perplexed. 'Lascar?'

'That is what we call east Africans, who work on the
boats. Anyway, I found him in Gravesend at the market
and questioned him. He did not want to say too much but
eventually he admitted that a boy had been taken on board
at Rouen, and had left the ship by rowing boat, just outside
Gravesend. So, our assumption has proved correct.' She
proffered a weak smile.

'That is good, we know now that we have not been wasting time. What more did he say?'

I cleared my throat.

'Very little, but I think that is all he knew. The other thing that has occurred is the old seaman – Jack Carter – changing his story about the rowing boat coming ashore, but I am fairly sure that he has been got at by Lynch. That man is dangerous. He might come after me next.'

She took some while to take this in, sipped some more coffee, then said, 'Then William, we must be careful. I will pass this information onto our people at Chislehurst – I am hopeful Louis will provide me with the ransom amount.'

I noted that her maid Antonia looked uneasy at this but kept her mouth shut.

Marie continued, 'William, when the time comes to exchange gold for Pierre, will you be there to help? I cannot do it, and I'm afraid Louis might not wish it to be seen that the French court is involved.'

'Of course, I will. Anything to help get your son back.'

She reached over and gently touched my hand. 'Thank you so much.'

I noted that this act of tenderness did not go unnoticed by Antonia, who by now was frowning.

'Excuse me madam but surely all decisions on paying the ransom and who is involved must be agreed with the Emperor.'

There was a stony silence; Marie was clearly angered at this intrusion.

'I think Antonia that you had best realise your position in the household. In fact, I am finding your presence here unhelpful. I would be grateful if you could pack your bags and return to Chislehurst. Immediately.'

Antonia looked shocked for a moment then regained her composure; clearly she would not be that heartbroken about leaving Marie and was probably more comfortable back in the security of the French court at Camden Place.

'Very well, Madam. I will pack immediately.' At this she curtseyed and left the table.

Marie looked at me, then after a few seconds whispered, 'I'm glad she is going. I find her presence unnerving. Will you telegram ahead and arrange for her to be picked up from the station?'

I nodded. 'Of course.' Then added, 'Will you be alright without her?'

'Of course, she is as good as useless. But Louis thought I should not travel on my own. Now is there anything else?'

I thought for a brief second then decided to take my chance.

'Marie, do you know it is Waterloo Day today and that there will be celebrations in the town tonight?'

She pulled a face.

'William, is this some sort of joke? Why should I, the lady-in-waiting to Empress Eugenie , wife of Napoleon Bonaparte's nephew, celebrate Waterloo Day?'

I stuttered a little.

'Sorry, I was not trying to be funny. It is just that I have had a tip-off that sailors from the ships will be rolling tar barrels down the street, just after sunset tonight. So, it could be quite dangerous if you didn't realise what was going on and got in the way.'

She smiled more deeply.

'William, I am only teasing you. But why would we wish to see this?'

'It may be that some of the sailors pushing the barrels might include seaman from the *Spirit of Rochester*? Maybe even John Lynch himself.'

Her eyes lit up.

'Yes, indeed it might be a chance to see that awful man in the flesh; that is settled then, you will meet me here at nine and escort me down to the high street. If anyone sees us we will pretend we are a courting couple on a night out – that will cause less suspicion than a woman on her own. Are we agreed?'

I was more than pleased by this turn of events.

'Certainly, Marie. Nine o'clock it is.'

At that I gently kissed her outstretched hand. 'I'll go and get the telegram off – shall I take Antonia to the station?'

Marie smiled 'That would be most helpful.' I bade au revoir and having sent off the telegram, returned twenty minutes later. Antonia was by now standing on the hotel steps. I quickly procured a hansom cab and took her to Gravesend station. We sat together in the cab in silence. Finally, she broke it.

'Mr Reeves, you realise that Marie is just one of many mistresses of Louis? He will not pay the ransom for a bastard son; of that you can be sure.'

Having said her piece, I let the silence return. She was a nasty piece of work and I was only too glad to see her depart onto the London-bound train.

I quickly forgot about Antonia and got my thoughts back to the only woman in my life. Walking back from the station to the Eagle, I could not help but admit that I had a distinct new spring in my step at the thought of being on Marie's arm tonight.

SIXTEEN

Bonfires for Waterloo

I arrived at the Clarendon at nine o'clock. It was a hot and humid evening. Marie greeted me in reception. She looked stunning, but pleasingly not overdressed. She spoke first.

'So, William you are ready for a night on the town – celebrating your Waterloo Day?'

I smiled.

'All a bit unfortunate I know but perhaps we can get a closer look at Lynch and his henchmen.'

I took her arm and we left the front door of the hotel and stepped out into the street. To anyone's eyes we looked like a typical courting couple, out for an evening promenade. We crossed the road in front of the hotel and stood for a while, looking out over the river. It was a good position to see over the town's riverfront. Looking to the west we could see the town pier, the Three Daws inn and beyond it the King's Arms and Eagle. At anchor, and close to the town pier, was the *Spirit of Rochester*, still in port. Beyond the riverfront and boats and colouring the river with its reddening light, a sunset was emerging along the Thames towards London. Not the greatest of sunsets as the humid conditions made it less than perfect, but a sunset none the less. I ventured to pass my opinion on this panorama.

'It's a good view from here. Though I am surprised that Lynch's boat is still here, moorings on this bit of the riverfront are at a premium usually.'

'Yes, it is strange. Do you think it is because of Pierre? Is Lynch staying here until he gets the ransom?'

I shook my head; I genuinely had not got a clue.

'Who knows?' At this I mopped my brow slightly with my hand as the warm humidity was getting to me.

'Now, now William you need a proper handkerchief for that.' Marie then produced a lace cloth from her sleeve and gently mopped my brow with it. Although she probably had not meant this to be a loving gesture, her feminine charm made everything she did gracious and often, unwittingly, sensuous.

'Thank you.'

She looked at the sky and at the darkening clouds obscuring the sunset. The light was peculiar now; it had a kind of alizarin red hue to it which felt more menacing than colourful. She spoke with a note of caution in her voice.

'It is very humid tonight, perhaps we will get rain soon?'

'Perhaps we will. Shall we walk up the high street to get a vantage point of the festivities?'

At that I took her arm again and we walked along the riverside to the Three Daws inn, at the junction with the high street. We then walked up the high street and noted how busy the town was tonight. There were a few inns along this thoroughfare and every one of them appeared to be full of sailors and townspeople. There was a party atmosphere in town with much raucous shouting and laughter, and drinkers spilling out into the street. We continued up the street taking this atmosphere in and near the top, just past the market entrance, we noticed that sailors were manoeuvring barrels into position. They were in no great hurry. Waiting, I presume, for the dusk and darkness before starting the barrel rolling.

I gently manoeuvred Marie over to the side of the street, where we were partially hidden by a projecting wall. I did not want us to be seen by anyone we knew, particularly Lynch himself. There was time to talk before the event started so I broached the subject of Marie's past.

'Marie, can I ask a little more about yourself? If that is not too forward.'

'Of course, William, ask me anything you like.'

'Tell me about the war, the siege of Paris, anything to give me a better idea of what you've been through.' She spoke openly to me; it seemed as if being away from the stuffy pomposity of the Clarendon, some weight had been lifted off her shoulders.

'I can only tell you what I know. I have been a member of Emperor Napoleon's court for almost fifteen years. Both before and after I had Pierre. Louis was exceedingly kind to me. As you know France was a powerful nation with a great empire. Colonies all over the world, great riches, everything. Louis rebuilt Paris, you know. Made it into a fine modern city. Then things went wrong, maybe he had – what you say – too many fingers in too many pies? Finally, we went to war with Prussia and he was betrayed at the battle at Sedan by his cowardly men. We knew then that our days in the Tuileries in Paris were over. The Prussians took Louis as a prisoner and moved him into house arrest in Cassel. I later joined him there, along with some of the loyalist people in his court. We were all virtually imprisoned, so could not travel back to France. We spent the whole winter as prisoners in Prussia. Then this March we were released, and Louis came to England bringing his loyal courtiers with him. Including myself. Louis' wife, Eugenie, had escaped Paris in September, just after Sedan, and was already in exile in England. Since we arrived in Chislehurst I have been making enquiries as to what happened to my son, and that is where Gordon and you come into it. That is my story.'

I sucked in the warm humid air and responded with as much confidence as I could muster.

'Somehow, in some way, we will find Pierre and bring him back to you. I promise that.'

She smiled, and tears began welling up in her eyes.

'Thank you, William, you are a good man.'

We looked at each other in the half light of dusk. I knew I had to get back to business and leave my feelings for Marie until the drama was over. I looked down the street. There were people everywhere and the inns and shops facing onto the narrow street now had their gaslights on, and there were faces pressed up against the windows staring out. The people were clearly waiting to see the festivities begin and there was a buzz of excitement. The street was now even narrower than usual because of the throngs of spectators on either side and darkness was now overtaking the last rays of sunlight. This was a dead straight thoroughfare running downhill to the riverside – and probably only ten feet clearance had been left in the centre of the road, presumably to allow the barrels through. All in all, it felt quite theatrical: the excitement before the curtain rises.

Then I saw him.

John Lynch.

The grey-haired old sea dog with an entourage in tow.

He was striding up from the pier where his boat was still moored. I gently tapped Marie on the shoulder.

'Look, that's him.'

She looked over and was clearly taking him in. He was wearing his captain's uniform and by his actions, and the demeanour of those around him, you could see he was the man very much in charge. The other officers in his group were clearly there just to do his bidding. Gently taking Marie's hand, I stepped her back into a nearby alleyway entrance, so that we could not be seen so easily. Now closer to her, I could smell her perfume. It smelt of roses, of summer, of woman. I smiled at her. Our eyes met for a brief moment but then she switched off and returned to the business in hand. She scrutinised Lynch and his gang.

'So that is Captain Lynch is it? He looks like a very mean man. I would happily kill him with my hatpin. Just like that.' She made a stabbing movement with her clenched hand. 'But that wouldn't get my son back, I know that – so, I will wait.'

It was now getting closer to the time of the lighting of the barrels. Perhaps thirty feet away from us a powerful fire had been lit in a brazier, placed in the middle of the street. It glowed red and orange in the darkness, lighting the faces of those around it. I noticed half a dozen young sailors holding unlit torches, then they excitedly, but meticulously, took turns to put their long torches into the flames of the brazier. With the torches alight I could now see the sailors more clearly and noticed that one of the sailors was Asif. He and the others then turned their attention to the tar barrels. Asif's job seemed to be to hold the barrel in place to prevent it rolling away. Then another sailor lit ragged cloths at either end of the keg, with the blazing torch. The barrels started to burn, first from one end, then from both. There were now in total four barrels all alight, lined up ready to be rolled down the street – clearly they were getting ridiculously hot, but Asif and the other sailors still held them firm, waiting for the signal. I could see then that it was Lynch who would be doing that. He seemed to take pleasure in getting his boys to hold onto the barrels forever, even though their hands must be burning.

Finally, he dropped a handkerchief – and the barrels were pushed away and started rolling down the street. Asif's job was now to run alongside one of the barrels and keep patting it to keep it going straight, but not too fast too soon. For the first chain or so, everything went fine, the crowd were cheering, all was well. Then, I could see the barrel beginning to escape his grasp. The weight and speed of it was too much for him to control! Thus, the inevitable happened – he had to let the barrel go. The flaming keg had escaped his grasp and was now gaining speed, and quickly, as it trundled down the steeply sloping street. The spectators shrank back from the flaming barrel as it raced past them. The other three-barrel gangs stopped moving and despite the heat, held the barrels firm against the slope. Asif's barrel was now hurtling down the street out of control. This created both uproarious shouting from onlookers, mixed with fear that it might head towards them! After about sixty yards, it was all over. The barrel veered to the right, hit a projecting wall, and stopped dead. The local innkeepers, who had clearly seen all this before, ran out with buckets of water and quickly smothered it. I could see immediately that Asif was mortified, and I soon realised why. Lynch, seeing this failure to roll the barrel straight, strode out across the street and gave him a massive kick between his legs. Asif doubled up in pain.

'You useless lascar, you can't even do what your told.' Asif stumbled back onto the side of the street apologising profusely. As he did so Lynch calmly walked back across the street to his vantage point. The festivities continued with the three remaining barrels walked down the street surrounded by the torchlit sailors. There was much applause for this. The crowds then followed the procession.

Marie and I could see there was safety and anonymity in numbers, so also joined the throng and followed them.

About fifty yards short of the end of the street the tar barrels were allowed to roll away. Whether this was pre-planned, or a spur of the moment decision, I do not know. They rolled fairly straight, following the street direction, though worryingly gaining speed as they went. Finally, inevitably, they crashed into the wall at the bottom. Just in front of the Three Daws. The tar was ablaze, but nobody seemed particularly concerned. Soon the local people and sailors, armed with buckets of water, extinguished the flames, and brought the light show to an end. There was much shouting and some applause. Despite the presence of Lynch, I had also been impressed and excited by the spectacle. So, I smiled at Marie, she smiled back at me. Then something strange happened.

I was suddenly aware that the spectators alongside the high street were now looking beyond the tar barrel cremation and the Three Daws, to the river beyond. The Thames at this time of night should have been just a velvet black backdrop, but instead I could see a distinct fire out in the river, on one of the dark silhouettes floating in the humid stillness. A cry went up from the crowd.

'It's the *Spirit of Rochester*, she's on fire!'

I looked down the street and saw John Lynch suddenly convulsed into action. He was shouting at his men to get back to the ship immediately. His lackeys were soon running hell for leather, back towards the pier whilst he bellowed out his orders.

We, along with what seemed half the population of Gravesend, watched on. The spirit was a timber clipper, so a fire, any fire, could be lethal. The ship's crew seemed to get back on board quickly and we could see them beating back the flames with brooms and dowsing them with buckets of water dredged out of the Thames.

Things still looked serious. Such a blaze on a timber vessel could easily prove terminal. Then, a remarkable thing occurred. We saw a blazing white lightning bolt, which illuminated the street like a thousand limelight's. This was almost immediately followed by a fierce clap of thunder. Within seconds torrential rain was cascading down on us. Whether this was a sign from God, or just luck, the heavy rain, along with the frantic crew, were putting out the main fire on the boat fairly quickly. Seeing the excitement was over, and getting more drenched by the second, we took shelter outside the Three Daws under the building's overhanging eaves. I looked at Marie to see if she was alright. Outside, in the darkness, she seemed somehow smaller, more vulnerable. She smiled. It was a pleasure to feel Marie alongside me. I knew I had feelings for her but didn't really know yet if they would be reciprocated. She smiled again.

'Well this a strange turn of events, William. Lynch's boat on fire. Perhaps it is God's work?' I looked at her. Did she know something I did not?

Just as I was musing as to what to do next, my thoughts were disturbed by a familiar voice nearby. Standing not twenty feet away from us, but out of sight by the inn entrance, was Jack Carter. He was showing his age and inebriation by pissing into the gutter and talking very loudly to some other old lag.

'Call that a fire, I could put that out with my own piss. I remember when this place was full of timber schooners. When they went up, they went up, not like that. It's already pretty much been put out. You know who I blame for it – the French, they have got their spies here in Gravesend. Did you know that? People working for Napoleon III. He is living in England, believe it or not. Fancy giving a bloody Napoleon sanctuary! His whore is staying at the Clarendon – not a lot of people know that. You can bet your life that she is behind it.'

At that I could feel Marie lunge forward, I grabbed her and put my hand over her mouth. She was clearly, and rightly, infuriated. Carter continued.

'Still that's what the country is coming to. This government's too soft. I know all about the French, my father was at Trafalgar, that is when we had real men at sea. Now it's just a bunch of unskilled chancers running the Navy. Come on, let us get another drink.' At that he and his companion, having completed their ablutions, returned back inside the bar. I looked at Marie questioningly; she was incandescent with rage, so any further questioning was out of the question. She barked at me.

'Take me back to the hotel, I've had enough of this hellhole for one night.' I meekly submitted to her request. Things had now gone a little frosty, the romance of hiding from the torrential rain was long gone. We walked back to her hotel in silence. The rain bucketed down, but she did not seem to care about getting wet.

Just before we got back to the Clarendon I got a good sight of the *Spirit* over the riverside green. The fire was now out, though some damage had been done. I ventured to comment.

'If somebody was trying to burn down the boat, they didn't make much of a job of it. They set the fire at the wrong end. If they had set it against the prevailing westerly wind the boat would be a burnt-out wreck by now.'

She said nothing: we got to the porch of the hotel and finally found shelter from the rain. She was clearly still upset.

'Thank you William, I'm sorry that our night was spoilt, but I'm nobody's whore. I only respect a man who would die for my reputation. I bid you goodnight.'

At that she was gone, and I stood alone; a chance had been presented to me to show my true feelings and I had missed it and missed it by a mile. I trudged home to the Eagle feeling deflated.

I did not sleep well that night. There is nothing worse than knowing you had something precious in the palm of your hand, only to let it fly away due to your own stupidity and indecision. My mind raced through ways I could repair the damage to our friendship, but I knew in my heart that the only thing that might win her back was if I rescued her son. Frankly, I did not have a clue how to achieve that either.

PART 2

The Emperor's Woman

SEVENTEEN
Another Day

I MUST HAVE FALLEN OFF to sleep very late but was woken again by the sound of the brewery dray horses clattering along the road. I reluctantly got out of bed and looked out the window. There was John Bennett walking down the street again, his walking stick tapping the ground as he went to the King's Arms. Every day he did this. Did they give him a bacon sandwich or something? Surely the last thing a publican wants is to be civil first thing in the morning.

I decided to go out for a walk along the riverside. The remains of the tar barrels were still in the street by the Three Daws. I walked on down to the promenade from where I could get a good sight of the *Spirit of Rochester*. I could see much activity on board. You could still smell the remains of last night's fire and charring and damage to the brow of the ship was evident. A small iron-sided steam tugboat was now in situ and a hawser had been attached to the old timber clipper. I watched for a while and finally both boats departed with the tug pulling the *Spirit* in her wake. She was heading due east down the river and I can only assume that some emergency repairs were to be undertaken. How this would affect the kidnap situation was anyone's guess. As the boats passed me I caught sight of Lynch pacing the decks, barking out orders. So at least I knew where he would be today.

I found a bench and sat for a while staring out over the water towards Tilbury Fort on the north bank. What was I to do now? Go to the Clarendon and beg forgiveness? Go back to the Eagle and hide under the bedclothes? Finally, I decided to visit Gordon, perhaps he might have some sage advice for me.

I arrived at the fort a few minutes later and asked for him. Unusually, I was asked to wait. It was a long wait and a full half hour before I was escorted into his sparse office. His greeting was a little dry today.

'Hello, Reeves, sorry you had to wait. What can I do for you?'

I hesitated to speak; he gestured for me to sit down.

'Thank you for seeing me sir. I noticed that there had been a fire on board the *Spirit of Rochester*, I wondered whether you had any more information on what occurred?'

He stood up and paced the room.

'Yes, indeed, a bit of a rum do. Appears the boat caught fire about ten o'clock last night. No serious damage but it has been towed to a dockyard on the Medway, near Strood, for repairs. Likely to only be out of action for a few days. Could have been a lot worse.'

I nodded. 'Yes, indeed the whole boat could easily have gone up. Any idea if it was an accident or arson?'

Gordon seemed a little awkward at this point and failed to look me in the eyes.

'We have no idea Reeves what happened. However, very unfortunately, a rumour is now racing around the town that it was caused by French agents working for Napoleon.'

'Surely not, that is ridiculous. How could such a rumour have got around?'

Gordon sighed. 'It does not matter if it is true or not, the problem is that this rumour is gaining traction. It even includes the information that Napoleon's lady-in-waiting is staying at the Clarendon – and is behind all of it.'

I was dumbfounded. I had heard what Jack Carter had said to his sidekick but could not understand why people believed it.

'So, what do we do about this rumour?'

'Action has already been taken, Reeves. I telegrammed Napoleon himself, to make him aware of the situation. He has responded by taking Marie-Anne back to Chislehurst – she left the Clarendon half an hour ago. Sorry about that but it was the only way to quash the rumour before things got out of hand. You understand?'

I was still struggling for words.

'But where does that leave the kidnap investigation? What am I supposed to do now?'

Gordon tried his best to give me a fatherly smile. 'I really don't know Reeves. Perhaps you need to go away and think about your next moves.' At that he sat back down at his desk and started looking at his large pile of papers that covered it. This was clearly an indication that my time was up. I bade him farewell and walked out back into the clear blue skies of Gravesend.

It was a beautiful day, but I felt devastated. Had I lost Marie for good? Would she never leave Chislehurst again?

Would I ever see her again? It was so painful. This sense of loss, though in truth she had only been in my life but a few days. I walked back down West Street feeling very downcast. Then as I passed the Three Daws I saw a familiar face; it was Asif, sweeping up the remains of last night's tar barrels.

'Asif, what are you doing here? I saw your boat leave for the Medway only an hour ago.'

He stopped sweeping and looked at me dejectedly.

'Sorry Mr Reeves, I have been thrown off the boat. Captain Lynch displeased with me.' He looked almost broken hearted. 'I am just tidying up for something to do. If I behave myself, the captain says he might take me back when boat returns.'

'So, where are you staying? Have you got any money to tide you over?'

He remained robust despite his sadness. 'I will be alright sir; I will get by.'

I was not too sure of this. 'Let me buy you breakfast at least.'

He smiled and agreed; putting his broom to one side, we set off up the high street to the market, where there were numerous cheap eating places. We found a fairly unimposing tearoom. It was a cheap place, but I was cautious of taking a lascar to anywhere more salubrious, as we might not have got served. To make sure all would be well, I ordered and paid for the food and led Asif to a table and chairs away from prying eyes and ears. 'Now Asif, I believe you to be a very decent man. Would you be able to help me in my enquiries about the missing French boy?'

He gestured by holding his hands out with palms upwards.

'I have told you everything I know Mr Reeves.'

I stopped him. 'Please call me William. Is there anything at all that you can remember of the events last September, when your boat came into Gravesend after sailing from France?'

He shook his head. 'Not really, we picked up the boy in Rouen. That was along with a cargo of flints. He was taken below and didn't come out again until we were approaching Gravesend. Just before we got to the town, out on the Hope, he was brought up from below and put in a rowing boat with two of the crew. They rowed him towards the shore, I could not really see much as it was too dark. So, I could not be sure of the direction they took but I assumed they were heading for the shore somewhere to the east of the town.'

I thought on this, then questioned him further. 'Would it be possible for you to judge where the *Spirit of Rochester* was at that time, and the direction the rowing boat went in?'

He replied instantly. 'Yes, sir, Master William, I will do my best.'

I smiled. 'Good, and what were the tidal conditions on the night?'

'It was a high tide with westerly wind that evening.'

'Good, the next high tide here today is late afternoon. Would you be willing to take me in a rowing boat following the route it took on that night?'

Asif perked up at this. Being on the sea, even in a rowing boat, was obviously his happiest domain.

'Yes Mr William, we could try, though I cannot promise to get it right.'

I knew this was a course of action worth undertaking. 'I trust you Asif to do your best. Can you meet me beside the river in front of the fort at four o'clock this afternoon?'

He smiled and agreed. We finished our food and parted company. I returned to the fort to arrange the boating trip with Gordon. Though not convinced by my idea, he agreed to obtain a rowing boat that afternoon and then surprised me by offering to come on board to experience the journey for himself.

EIGHTEEN

The Boat Ride

As AGREED, AT FOUR O'CLOCK, I was back at the small jetty in front of the fort – Asif was already there. The boat owner clearly did not believe Asif, or I, had any authority, so he waited until Gordon arrived to hand over the boat. I introduced Gordon to Asif, who seemed unfazed by my new friend.

The boat was a small affair capable of being oared by a single person. Asif was clearly keen to do this, so we gave him the oars and took our seats shakily at the back of the boat. I was glad it was a warm summer afternoon and almost windless. I asked Asif to take us to the approximate position of the *Spirit* when the rowing boat was launched. He took us out into the Thames, perhaps 200 yards offshore and 400 yards downriver, just outside the town. As we gently eased our way out into the river I could see what a busy little port Gravesend was, the shipping passing by was continuous and I was concerned that the wash from the big ships travelling fast up the river might capsize us. They would scarcely see our rowing boat until it was too late. Luckily, the wind was little more than a breeze and from the usual prevailing direction – blowing from the south-west. The only other problem was the tide itself, which could be deceptively strong. Luckily, Asif seemed a very accomplished rower and was very much in charge of the direction and speed of the boat.

On the way we made some small talk to lighten the atmosphere; I asked Asif why he had become a seaman. It appeared that he had left Zanzibar, where his family had been textile merchants, due to a business dispute. Lynch's boat docked at Zanzibar en route from India, with a cargo of spices, and took on several lascars as crew. He had been sailing with him ever since, mostly doing the clipper tea runs from India and China, but ever since the opening of the Suez Canal killed that trade off, doing any work that was going. Hence the flint run from Rouen to the pool of London.

Finally, he stopped rowing and we drifted to a halt, not in midstream but far enough away from the shore to feel vulnerable. 'This is about where the *Spirit* was anchored that night, sir.'

Gordon seemed pleased at the accuracy of Asif's memory and pressed him further. 'Thank you Asif, now can you take us in the direction the rowing boat took on the night last September.' Asif looked around for some time to find any bearings; at length he set our rowing boat towards the shoreline on an east-south-easterly course. Reaching the shoreline was not that easy as the tide and current moved us around and veered us offline, but Asif rowed on regardless and within a few minutes we had reached a muddy beach.

It looked as if we were about a mile east of Gravesend, close to a place known as Denton. There was not that much at Denton, in fact the only discernible jetty was one leading to what looked like a salvage timber yard. Gordon seemed to know it, and I remembered it from my walk.

'This is Tibbalds' place. He was once a well-respected shipbreaker, specialising in breaking up the old prison hulks – now it is a more general woodyard. In fact, I think we may have bought some timber and stone here for the renovation works at the fort.'

We looked on. Could this be the place Pierre was brought to, and if so could he still be here? Gordon seemed to read my thoughts.

'I don't think it would be possible to hide a boy here for months. Just not practicable.' I looked over the site. Even from out on the river you could smell the hot tar and aged timber. The yard looked a mess, just a graveyard for old boats, broken up into a thousand pieces. At one end of the yard was a slightly tidier stack of timber and beyond that were what looked like wooden beer barrels.

I asked Gordon, 'Do you know if they have a cooperage here?'

'Yes, just one of their side-lines, I think they produce the barrels for the brewery in West Street. Is that important?'

I was thinking aloud. 'What if they kept the boy at the yard in secret, for a short while, then when it was time for him to be moved, hid him inside one of the barrels? They are certainly big enough. He could then be delivered anywhere. Perhaps to an inn cellar in the middle of nowhere?'

Gordon frowned. 'Well it's a theory at least, but where is the proof?' We looked at each other; neither of us clear as to what our next move was. Finally, Gordon came to a decision.

'Let us go and talk to Tibbalds, see if he knows anything.' At that we beached the boat and Asif jumped out to haul it up the mud and shingle beach. We also got out, trying all the while to keep our shoes and socks from getting soaked in the slimy mud. We asked Asif to stay with the boat while we took the 100 paces or so up to the breakers' yard. The entrance was open now but in the makeshift timber hut by the way in, there was nobody to be seen. Luckily at the other end of the yard we could see two coopers at work, making new barrels, so we walked over to them. Gordon did the talking.

'Good day gentlemen, is Tommy Tibbalds around?'

One of the coopers was just hammering in a hot metal hoop over the staves. He turned to us. 'Mr Tibbalds is not about today. Can I help you?'

Gordon thrust out a hand and introduced me, and himself. Then I piped up, 'We are interested in these beer barrels – what sort of quality are they?'

The cooper looked back.

'The finest sir, the best in Kent. We send them everywhere, all the breweries. Everyone knows they're the best.'

I smiled. 'Tell me, do you supply the kegs to the brewery on West Street in Gravesend?'

He did not hesitate. 'Certainly do sir. They are one of our biggest customers.' I was pleased that he was being so straight with us.

'We are interested in a load of kegs that was sent to the West Street brewery last September. Do you keep a record of your sales and deliveries?'

At this point the cooper's smile faded; he obviously didn't want to answer this.

'I do not do the sales side, sir. You would have to speak to Mr Tibbalds about that.' The other cooper had now stopped working and silently stared at us. The atmosphere was now growing frosty.

Gordon interjected, 'I can see that you are terribly busy, we will speak to Mr Tibbalds at some more convenient time. I bid you good day.' At that we turned and walked back to the boat. Gordon spoke as we got out of earshot. 'We will not find anything at the yard, you can bet on that. And I do not want to cross-examine Tommy Tibbalds today. I will get nothing out of him anyway. He is a big name around here, knows a lot of people. He also owns a chalk quarry down at Swanscombe – so he has got his fingers in a lot of pies. Best leave him alone till we have got more evidence. Let us get ourselves back to the fort.'

We got back to the boat and eased ourselves in, within seconds the adroit Asif had the boat in the water and his hands on the oars. I turned to Gordon. 'They know more than they are saying. I need to get a look at John Bennett's books to see if there was a delivery in late September.'

Gordon seemed unconvinced. 'It is just a theory Reeves, nothing more. Let us get back.'

At that, Asif began to row in long powerful strokes upriver towards Gravesend, now sticking close to the shore to avoid the larger boats and their wakes. Before long we were back to the New Tavern Fort and manoeuvring towards its small jetty. Just as we were about to disembark we caught sight of the mud larkers, messing about by the foreshore. I could see the boy I had spoken to a few days back, Fred, amongst them. Gordon shouted over to him.

'Come over here Fred, I've got something I need to know.' He seemed happy to oblige; obviously, Gordon was respected, maybe even loved, by Fred. Dragging his feet out of the mud he walked over to us. He was very dirty and smelly, but clearly happy in his work. Gordon continued, 'Now, you probably noticed that there was a fire on board the *Spirit of Rochester* boat last night, about ten o'clock. Did you see anything?' There was no response so Gordon asked the same question again to Fred, who was beginning to squirm.

'I didn't see nuffink sir, we had nothing to do with that fire.'

Gordon sighed. 'So where were you all at ten o'clock last night?'

'We was all back in the hostel in bed sir, fast asleep.' Gordon was now clearly getting agitated.

'Don't give me all that, you and the rest of the lads would never go to sleep while there are burning barrels to watch and crowds to pickpocket from. I know you were about. What did you see?'

Fred looked over to his mud larker friends who had now joined us. Nothing was said but a sense of guilt, of untold stories, pervaded the atmosphere.

'Very well let us go to my office in the fort – just you Fred, the others can go.' At that Gordon grabbed his collar and frog marched him towards his office in the fort. I followed meekly on with Asif, both of us unsure of the protocol in these situations. We hastily made our way through the fort and I gestured for Asif to stay outside Gordon's office, which he did.

Inside the office, Fred was forcibly sat down opposite Gordon. I stood by, watching. 'Now Fred, I am going to ask you one more time about your involvement in the fire, because I can sense you know more than you're saying. If you come clean on this, I will make sure you have a good meal tonight, if not I'll put you in the cells and you can starve.'

Fred was clearly discomforted by this news and squirmed in his seat. 'I didn't see nuffink sir.'

Gordon was not going to leave this. 'I understand you're frightened of repercussions, but you will not get into any trouble, we know the captain of the boat, John Lynch, as do you, and he is a horrible man, but without your help we cannot lay a finger on him. Now I'll ask the question again.'

Fred butted in. 'It's alright sir. I will tell the truth, it was me and the other boys, we hate Lynch's guts. He is a dirty bastard. We were hanging around last night and saw his boat almost empty, with all the crew watching the barrel rolling. It was so warm we all went for a swim. We could see there was no one on the boat, so we climb on – just for a bit of a lark. Nobody saw us, so we just messed around a bit, then I pulled down this lamp hanging from the rigging. So, for a laugh I was swinging it about, but then it fell off its hook and smashed on the ground and set some old sailing cloth alight. Before we know it, everything was on fire, so we dived back into the water before anyone noticed us. Don't know what happened to the ship's guard, we never saw him, probably pissed, if you excuse my language. We didn't mean no harm sir. It was just a lark. We never meant to drop the lamp and start a fire – honest.' Fred paused for breath and looked around sheepishly, fearing chastisement.

Gordon finally broke the silence. 'Thank you Fred for being so honest. Now you must realise that in normal circumstances I would have to report this to the constabulary and the ship's captain.'

Fred looked horrified at this. 'No, sir, please don't tell Mr Lynch, he would kill us.'

Gordon continued unabashed. 'However, on this occasion I will do neither. But, never, and I repeat, never, do this again. Am I clear?'

Fred could hardly get the words out quick enough.

'Yes, sir, certainly sir, never again, sir.'

'Alright, now go to the quartermaster and ask him to provide you, and the other boys, some tea and bread. That will be all.' Fred departed quickly with numerous 'Thank you sir, thank you's', as he left the room a much-relieved boy.

I sat down in the chair opposite Gordon.

'So, where do we go from here?'

'No idea Reeves, but at least we know what occurred last night.'

I looked back at him.

'So, does this mean we can kill the rumour about French spies burning down the ship?'

Gordon looked back at me like a parent to a naughty child. 'Of course not. To state that would mean giving up Fred to the authorities and I gave him my word I would not.'

I felt exasperated and outlined my concerns.

'The problem is that Marie-Anne is now back in Chislehurst, we need her here in Gravesend.'

He looked sternly at me, with a look of grim displeasure.

'You mean, you need her here! It has not passed my attention that you were seen out with Marie at the festivities last night, and my sources tell me that you and her looked, shall we say, close. Yes?'

I nodded. 'You do realise that if the ex-Emperor knew about this, your life would be probably cut short. He might be getting old and ill, but I am sure he feels very protective towards Marie – so you would be wise to not get involved and keep your feelings to yourself. Do I make myself clear?'

I knew he was right. 'Yes, of course – I will follow your advice.' Gordon seemed content at this and gestured that he wanted to get back to his work. I made one last request.

'Just one more thing, if I can ask you a favour. Asif has been thrown off his ship so is penniless and homeless. Can you give him a job and lodgings here at the fort?'

Gordon's kindness was undiminished, he replied without hesitation.

'Of course – the man has helped us; I can find him some labouring work and he can sleep within the fort. Is that all?'

I thanked him for his assistance and left.

NINETEEN

Bennett

I walked slowly back to the Eagle. I did not see Asif but assumed he was still somewhere in town. Just as I was passing the brewery, John Bennett appeared, he didn't see me and was walking in the opposite direction . The issue of the beer barrels was still on my mind; it might be a long shot, but could Pierre have been hidden in one from Tommy Tibbalds at Denton? Perhaps if I could find out if there had been a delivery of barrels from Tibbalds at the end of last September that might make a case for Pierre having been smuggled from the boat into a beer barrel – then brought to the brewery. From there he could be taken somewhere secluded and secure, perhaps. It was all conjecture, but it was all I had to go on. Perhaps I needed to visit Mr Bennett's office again, but at midnight and have a look through his ledgers? What secrets might they hold? I felt that I was making progress. If I could only find Pierre alive, then perhaps Marie would give me the time of day? That was my hope.

Instead of going back to the Eagle I strode off down the riverside towards the fort, taking in the sea breezes on this fine day. Within minutes I saw what I had come for. There was Fred and his fellow mud larkers, still working the muddy banks. I gestured for him to come over to me.

'Fred, I just wanted to say thanks for telling the truth back there with Gordon.'

He smiled. 'That's alright sir, he's a good bloke. We would do anything for him.'

I nodded in agreement. 'I would just like to pick your brains one more time, if I may?'

'Very well sir, but I don't think you'll find much more up there.'

'You know the brewery in West Street. Does it have an entrance round the back facing onto the river?'

Fred did not hesitate. 'Of course it does sir, that is where they unload stuff off boats and barges, instead of at the front.'

That is what I wanted to hear.

'Would it be easy to break into the brewery from the river side at night do you think?'

Fred nodded. 'Piece of cake sir. You can get into the building by jemmying open the back door to the river. Only trouble is they has a night watchman, Jessie Armitage, we know him because his son was one of us for a while, till he passed away. God bless his soul.'

I thanked Fred for his help, then let him get back to his work. I then walked into New Tavern Fort and was able to meet Gordon straight away. I broached the subject of the brewery and asked him about the night watchman, Mr Armitage.

'Yes, Jessie Armitage, we bumped into him on West Street. His wife died in childbirth and he developed a serious alcohol problem, lost his son as well. The poor boy had to live on the streets because Jessie could not look after him, or himself for that matter. Rumour is that he was murdered. Between you and me, there was also an inference that he had been used by sailors drinking at the King's Arms, for unspeakable practices. But the coroner had no evidence. So, it was death by drowning. Often happens to those mud larkers, they take silly risks to get stuff from the river bottom. Anyway, with God's help, we managed to get Jessie off the drink – and now he's back at the brewery, on probation, as a night watchman.'

I was taken aback by that story but could say nothing apart from how sorry I was for Armitage. I then told Gordon my plans for a midnight foray into Bennett's office. He thought for a moment, then replied briskly, 'Alright Reeves, you have my blessing. Be discreet though and no damage to the brewery. I will tip off Armitage that you are coming and recommend that he keeps his head down. Obviously if it all goes wrong, I know nothing. Is that clear?'

'Yes. Of course,' I replied. At that our meeting finished, I bade farewell and left Gordon's office, clear in my plans for that night.

I swiftly strode back towards the Eagle. As I rounded the corner into West Street I could see Asif standing by the streetlight looking a bit lost. 'Hello Asif, everything alright?'

He looked down at his feet and replied, 'I don't know Mr Reeves, sir, I'm used to being part of a crew, taking orders. I don't know what to do with myself without a ship.'

I could see he was a little distressed.

'Don't worry Asif, I have a little job you can help me out with tonight. Then tomorrow, I will see about finding a new boat for you to crew on. Is that alright with you?'

'That would be wonderful, Mr Reeves.'

I could see he was perfect for what I had in mind.

'This work does require you to do something a little illegal. I want to break into the brewery tonight to have a look around; is that alright with you?'

He looked more concerned at first, then said, 'That is fine with me Mr Reeves. Just tell me what I have to do.'

I reached into my pocket and brought out some florins and shillings.

'Can you go into town and buy a gemmy and anything else you can think of for opening doors, perhaps hair clips that can be bent into key shapes, things like that. Also, a bag to put them in?'

He nodded.

'Right then. Meet me down by the river at midnight… Just behind the Eagle is an alleyway which goes down to the river's edge, it will be low tide tonight. Make sure you are on time.'

Asif was clearly happy at this new adventure and scurried off into town with the silver coins plunged deep into his pockets.

TWENTY

Night Work

I MET HIM AS ARRANGED at midnight. All was quiet, and the tools of the trade were in his workman's bag. I had also procured a Davey lamp from Gordon's quartermaster.

'Ready,' I said.

We set off down the narrow alleyway that led to the foreshore. All was silent here, on this strip of shingle between the town and the great river. With nothing to see my sense of smell became more acute and I took in the mix of odours coming from the river – salt and seaweed and great age – this river had flowed past here forever.

It was low tide, and there was just enough moonlight to enable us to pick a route across the mud and shingle beach up to the brewery's external iron staircase. The noise of our footsteps on the shingle was our only company. The staircase was probably used in the past for deliveries by barges, now it was covered in slimy green weed, so I assumed it was no longer in use. We quietly one step at a time ascended the stairs and arrived at the back door of the building. All was quiet. I took the gemmy from Asif and started trying to work the door open, with little success. He gestured for me to let him have a go. Immediately he made an impression, working the corner of the door with the edge of his jemmy. Slowly but surely the door started to loosen out of its frame. Finally, with a discernible crunch, the timber frame was broken, and the door opened. We had made some noise, so both of us stood in silence for a short while, waiting to see if our presence had disturbed anyone. We could see a dim light inside the brewery, but no noise or movement. Asif touched his ear with a cupped hand. I listened more intently. Nothing, Jessie Armitage must have been in the porter's office but was turning a blind eye to us. I cautiously opened the door. We were now at the back of the cooperage and could smell horses nearby, probably in an adjoining stable, but they seemed to be undisturbed by our efforts. We crept through the cooperage, being careful not to trip over the tools or timber pieces on the floor and emerged in the main warehouse area. This was where the drays would be loaded with barrels every day, and I noted numbered bays which I assumed they used.

A dim light was coming from a small porter's office, which was located by the main double-height solid timber gates on the brewery's frontage to West Street. We crept up to the office and looked in. Yes, there he was – the watchman Jessie, reading a book, pretending to be unaware of our presence. We swiftly moved towards the foot of the iron staircase leading to John Bennett's office. By walking slowly, and with soft footsteps, we managed to make little noise and were soon at the top and facing the office door. Asif took the lead and started to pick the lock. He was clearly an expert and within seconds the door was open. I had brought with me the Davey lamp, and this gave off more than enough light to read any paperwork we might find.

While Asif kept guard I studiously studied the spines of the big leather-bound ledgers, stacked neatly on the high wooden shelves. The contents were written on the ledgers' spines, and I soon found one relating to keg purchases and sales. I hauled the heavy ledger off the shelf and gently placed it on the desk. I then carefully opened it and after some leafing through, found the right page. Yes, my theory was probably right. Written in ornate black script was the information I wanted, they had received a big delivery of new barrels from Tommy Tibbalds on the 22nd September 1870, exactly when I would have expected. Emboldened by this I carefully lifted the ledger back onto its shelf and turned to Bennett's desk. Without any delay Asif opened the desk drawers with his trusty hairpin. Holding the Davey lamp above, I carefully went through the drawer contents.

The items inside the desk were not surprising at first. Lots of paperwork that had little meaning to my investigation. One oddity was in the bottom drawer, where there seemed to be a good supply of bread and cheese. Who knows why, perhaps Bennett was so mean he bought in bulk and pigged out on it during the day? One other thing caught my eye. It looked unremarkable at first, but something told me to look further. It was a large, foolscap-size, sealed envelope with no writing on its cover. I gently opened it, so it could be resealed later. I expected to find some more documents related to shipping, or brewing, but instead to my surprise there were photographs. Dozens of them – dirty pictures, pornography. This was quite a shock. I showed them to Asif. We both had to stifle a giggle. However, as we looked at the individual pictures our humour was spent. This was not normal cheeky pictures of naked women, but overwhelmingly photographs of naked men and boys! These were shocking but then we realised that finding these photographs could be potentially good news for us. However, he had obtained these pictures, Bennett must in some way have broken decency laws in handling them. This could be the handle, the hook I needed to get information extracted from him.

Then, just as I was about to put the pictures back into the envelope, a hand-written invoice fell out. I put the lamp close to it and read the name: *Bussell Portraiture Studio, Harmer Street, Gravesend.* More luck. I now knew where these had originated from. It had been stupid of Bennett to retain the invoice but he no doubt thought his office desk was an impregnable castle where all his dirty little secrets could be hidden safely. I took a number of the most incriminating prints from the envelope, and the invoice, and then carefully replaced the remainder back in the envelope and placed it in the bottom of the drawer.

We then set about repairing our handiwork – closing the desk, tidying the ledgers, and leaving quietly through the office door – making sure it was shut behind us. We crept down the staircase. I could see Jessie in the office, so felt obliged to quietly put him in the picture. I softly knocked on the door and he stood up and slightly opened it.

'Did you get into the office without doing any damage?'

'Yes, no problems.'

Jessie seemed calmed by this. 'So, the story is: I heard a sound at the river door of it being forced open. I went to see what was happening, and the burglars must have heard me and run off without stealing anything?'

'Exactly. That way you will be in the clear Jessie.'

'That's a relief, I need to keep sweet with the brewery bosses. I still hope I can get back on the drays. I hate sitting here on my own all night.'

'I'm sure you will. Now we will bid you goodnight. You never saw us. We never saw you.' He nodded and we made our way towards the river door. We then retraced our steps, exiting through the back door out into the cool moonlit night. We had done it! I shook Asif's hand and bade him to depart. It was a job well done. Asif wandered off into the night and I quietly returned to my hotel room making sure I did not leave muddy footprints everywhere. We had achieved what I had wanted and, by chance, a lot more. I had the evidence I needed; that Bennett was probably connected to Pierre's disappearance, and instrumental in moving him around in a beer barrel. As a bonus, the pictures of boys showed he was rotten to the core and probably one of Lynch's inner circle. Despite the night's excitement, I slept well.

TWENTY-ONE

Gordon

NEXT DAY I WENT TO see Gordon at the fort. I now had all this information to share but was uncertain what to do with it. In normal circumstances I might have taken it direct to the constabulary, fingering both Bennett and the photographer, but my job was to find Pierre, simple as that.

Gordon saw me immediately. On walking in I could see his desk had a copy of the local paper on it; for once he seemed in a cheerful mood.

'Hello Reeves. Good news. The *Gravesend Chronicle* have run with the story I leaked to them.' He handed me the paper on whose front page was an article about the fire on board the *Spirit*. I read it quickly and could see the gist of it was that the blaze had been an accident – caused by over-adventurous, unknown kids, swimming out to the boat and accidentally knocking over a lantern. I smiled. He was clearly incredibly pleased and continued.

'That has killed off the French spies rumour – without putting Fred and his mud larkers in the dock. A good day's work, don't you think?'

I was pleased as well and thought I might take advantage of his obvious good mood.

'Does this mean, that as the French connection is now discounted, I can bring Marie back to Gravesend to help with my enquiries?'

Gordon's mood changed quickly. He scoffed, 'I did not do this to help your love life Reeves! This was all about politics and the need to avoid an international embarrassing incident.' I could see he meant what he said, so left it at that.

'So, Reeves, what else have you to impart today?'

I paused then, came clean about last night's events.

'I needed to gather more information and try to prove my theory about the beer barrels was plausible. So, I visited the brewery late last night and managed to enter John Bennett's office. I then went through his paperwork and found some things of interest in his desk.'

'This is what I found in his desk.' I took the photographs out and laid them on the desk in front of him.

'There are just a few here. I left the rest in the hope he does not know they are missing.'

Gordon looked at the photographs with total dismay and disgust. In front of him were pictures of naked boys.

'My God Reeves, this is filth, debauchery – I cannot look at them.' At that he turned the pictures over and sat back down in his chair, obviously shaken. He sat like that for a few seconds then carefully chose his words.

'So, Reeves we now know that Mr Bennett is a wicked man. Almost certainly with ungodly homosexual tendencies. A truly disgusting individual.'

I concurred with him and offered some more information.

'Also, the pictures were taken at a local studio, in Harmer Street. There was an invoice in the box. So, the photographer is also guilty of horrendous practices.' Gordon was still red-faced with anger. 'Don't worry Reeves, by the time this affair is over the photographer will never work again unless it is in a prison workshop. This is filthy business to be involved in.' I agreed with him and continued.

'Yes, it is truly disgusting, but I have to ask you Gordon. Do you recognise any of the boys? Might they have gone to your school or used the night shelter at some time?' Gordon picked up the photographs again, as if handling turds, and put them picture-side up. He looked through the stack.

'No Reeves, I don't. My guess is that they have been brought in from London. In some ways I hope they are boys used to this lifestyle and not good God-fearing boys dragged off the streets against their will.'

We sat in silence for a while, which Gordon finally broke.

'So, what do you want to do next? Shall we take this information to the Kent constabulary?'

I looked him in the eye.

'No, I would rather not at this time. I need this information as leverage on Bennett, and perhaps the photographer as well, to find Pierre and bring him back safe and sound.'

Gordon seemed to agree with this. 'Very well, I'll leave it to you as to how to proceed but keep me informed.' I carefully put the photographs back into the envelope and bade farewell to Gordon.

I then scurried down to the post office to send a telegram to Marie asking her to come back to Gravesend immediately.

TWENTY-TWO

Marie Comes Back

THE NEXT MORNING, I RECEIVED the information I wanted. Marie would be arriving on the two o'clock train from London. I set off in good time and strode up the high street towards the station.

Oddly, the busy streets full of shoppers and workers of all kinds made me feel lonely. Perhaps the photographs had upset me more than I knew. I thought back on my life and all the changes that had ensued since I was a boy. Back then there were no trains, no telegraph, few factories, and people relied on candles for light. Most folk were born and died in the same village. Now everything had changed, and was still changing, fast.

This inner soul-searching was making me think more about Marie. I knew I was highly attracted to her, maybe even in love, but where did I stand? It would have been clearly wrong to have such feelings for a married woman, but what of a mistress? I had heard that in France every man of means has a mistress and often these women were highly educated and loyal to their married lovers. Was it morally wrong to have lust for another man's mistress? In any case Napoleon's health was now so bad I assume that Marie was mistress in name only. So, would it be morally right for me to take this further? I was still pondering these thoughts when I arrived at the station, at the top end of the high street, and bought a platform ticket.

The station was a good size and heavily used with some people travelling to London every day for work. The railway had been built fifteen feet under the level of the streets, so the trains emerged through a chalk cutting into the station. This clever planning made the railway almost invisible to the town above.

I stood on the platform and awaited the train from London. It soon arrived, dead on time, in a cloud of smoke. The train gently slowed to a halt. I waited for the passengers to open their compartment doors and it was with much relief and joy that I saw Marie standing at the carriage door. She seemed to be on her own and had no luggage, no Antonia this time, thank goodness! I swiftly strode over to her and holding her hand gently, but firmly, helped her down the train step onto the platform. It felt like I was half of a married couple, meeting after a separation.

'I'm so glad you could make it, Marie.'

She smiled. 'No, it is you I must thank for keeping me informed and not giving up. Can we go to a tearoom?'

I smiled. 'Of course. There is one just over the street.'

At that we walked side by side through the station barrier onto the high street, and across the road into the tearooms. Although not as luxurious as the Clarendon, it was more than adequate, with clean tablecloths and waitress service.

We found a good table in the corner away from prying ears. I gently pulled the seat out for her and she daintily sat down. I then took my seat opposite her and opened the conversation.

'I'm afraid it's not quite as comfortable as the Clarendon.'

She smiled. 'Dear William, I have taken refreshments in a thousand times worse places in Paris.' I smiled but felt almost lost for words and awkward.

'How was your journey?'

'It was nice; I was far more relaxed being on my own without that awful woman Antonia.'

I was a little surprised by the sharpness of her reaction. 'I thought you two got on?'

She gave me a long look, then scoffed, 'You have no idea what it is like to be surrounded by people who despise you. For all her smiles, Antonia did not like me. It is the same at Chislehurst. My only friend is Louis – who is away in hospital most of the time. Eugenie mistrusts me, and the other staff follow her lead by making me feel unwanted.'

At that moment, the waitress came to our table .She was clearly in a rush and this made her face blush. 'Sorry to keep you waiting, sir.' She stood poised with her pad and pencil. I tried to order coffee and scones, but the waitress was quick to inform me they did not serve coffee. We made do with tea instead, which I knew Marie hated.

The waitress scurried off and Marie continued, 'Now, what is the news you wish to tell me?'

I shuffled in the seat, unsure where to begin but did so anyway.

'On the day after the Waterloo celebrations, I met with Gordon again. Later the same day I met the lascar who worked on Lynch's ship, Asif is his name, and he is a thoroughly decent chap. Now, I probed his memory of that fateful night in September when the *Spirit* came to Gravesend. He could just about remember the course taken by the rowing boat that left the ship on that night. So, we retraced its course, and it did appear to lead to a woodyard in Denton, run by a man called Tommy Tibbalds. The yard is located about a mile down the river. Now, one of Tibbalds' little businesses is making beer barrels. I also found out he delivers the completed kegs to the brewery in West Street, Gravesend. So, it occurred to me, what if Pierre had been brought ashore at the woodyard, and hidden in a beer barrel? He could then be transported to a more secure location without anyone knowing.'

She looked long and hard at me.

'But this is only a theory William, there is no proof, we are no further on.' I could see her desperation but carried on regardless.

'That is what I thought, so I decided to raid the shipping agent's office at night in the hope of finding some paperwork linking a barrel delivery to Pierre's disappearance.' She seemed to have a shadow of a smile now, so I continued.

'Anyway, myself and Asif broke into the brewery and managed to get inside John Bennett's office. We opened his desk drawer and found not only the invoice for a barrel delivery in September – a few days after Pierre landed – but also some incriminating photographs.' I hesitated for a moment.

'Photographs, William, what sort of photographs?'

The tea and scones arrived, so I stopped for a moment, waiting for the waitress to do her duties. After she had gone I spoke quietly to Marie.

'The truth is they were dirty pictures, pornography. Mostly naked men but also- I was stumbling over my words slightly; this was awkward, she could see my predicament and stepped in.

'Do not be shy William, remember I was the Emperor's mistress. Nothing will shock me.'

'There were pictures of boys as well.'

She gasped. 'Not my Pierre?'

'No, not Pierre. Good Lord no. We don't know where the boys came from, but we do know where they were photographed. Tucked away in the envelope was an invoice from a studio in Harmer Street, here in Gravesend. So, the pictures had clearly been taken there.' She sat back slightly, taking all this in. I then carefully poured tea through a strainer into our china cups. She looked at the brown brew with disdain.

'William, why does nobody appreciate coffee in your country? Tea always tastes like dishwater.' She clearly had lost her appetite. 'So, William, what do you suggest we do next?'

'I really don't know. We could go to the Gravesend constabulary and give them the information. They would certainly act against the studio, but it would be awkward admitting I had discovered this evidence through a burglary. Also, would it get us any closer to getting Pierre back?'

She thought for a moment. 'You are right. Let us leave the police out of this. We will go down to this studio ourselves now.' This course of action left me surprised and worried.

'Surely it would be unwise to confront the photographer with this evidence, that would be for the constabulary to do.'

She smiled. 'William, you are being too honest, too straightforward, you need to use your head more. We will go to the studio as a married couple who wish to have their portrait taken as a gift to my parents. That way we can see what kind of man this photographer is.' I could see her reasoning so agreed to this course of action. With this decided, we both relaxed.

'Please William, drink your tea, there is no hurry. We have time to talk. Tell me. Why are you not married at your age?' I was taken aback by this question but tried to answer honestly.

'I have just been too busy, and my line of work is so demanding and poorly paid, that taking on a wife would be difficult.' She sat back a little more in her seat and seemed to be almost flirting now.

'Perhaps it is because you have not found the right woman?'

I nodded. 'That is probably the real reason.'

'And your Lieutenant-Colonel Gordon, he is not married either?' I affirmed that he was not.

'Why do you think that is, William?'

'It is not for me to say but he seems married to his work and the Church. That is the sort of man he is.'

She smiled gently. 'Very well, I suppose he is an upright citizen who takes his work very seriously. We need people like that.' I took a sip or two of the tea. It was not that good. She could see that discussing my friend's sexuality was making me awkward.

'Shall we progress to the studio?' she said. I nodded and quickly paid the bill. We left the tearoom.

So, we were to be a married couple in the photographs. Was this my dream come true, or were we heading for more trouble?

Within five minutes' walk we were at the Gravesend Portraiture Studio in Harmer Street, its shopfront ,and name over the window in ornate black script *Bertrand Bussell Photographer* , seemed to proclaim it as a fine ,upstanding local business. We stepped inside and came face to face with the owner who introduced himself as Bertrand Bussell. He was middle aged with a fine handlebar moustache and a cheery, reddened, face. Probably a drinker.

I asked if it were possible that we could have a family photograph taken. He agreed immediately and said he could do it straight away. At that, after agreeing to the price, we were shown down a corridor to two small dressing rooms. His and hers, behind sash curtains. Mr Bussell suggested we make sure we were happy with our appearance, while he set up his camera and lighting in the adjacent studio. I entered the dressing room and looked around. Just a mirror and a dressing gown in the small place. I quickly adjusted my coat and hair to something half decent, then waited outside for Marie. She seemed to take longer than I expected but I knew it was not my place to hurry a lady. Finally, she emerged but to my shock her fine silk dress had gone, and she was only covered up by a dressing gown – my mouth dropped open. At that moment Mr Bussell appeared and without looking, said, 'Are we all set? He then caught sight of Marie and stopped in mid-sentence.

'Now Mr Bussell,' Marie said in her silkiest tones. 'I am afraid we have got you here under false pretences. You see my husband was too embarrassed to ask you this, but the truth is, he is in the colonial service and tomorrow sails for India. I would like some nice photographs of myself to remind him of all he is missing. I can see you are a man of the world who understands these things. No?'

Mr Bussell looked a little strained but had clearly had such requests before.

'Very well madame, but you must realise this is a family business. This matter must be strictly confidential. You understand?'

She smiled. 'Of course,' then turned to me. 'This will be something to remind you of me when you are alone on those long hot nights in India my dear.'

Mr Bussell looked at me. I realised I had no option but to go along with whatever game she was playing. 'Of course, my love, if that is what you want?'

She smiled deeply. 'It is. Now Mr Bussell, can we get on with this before I catch a chill? And also, would it be alright if my husband were in the studio while the pictures were taken?'

Bussell was now putty in her hands. 'Of course, whatever my client wants. I am merely your servant in this matter.'

We then proceeded into his studio space with Marie in front. I stood behind Bussell and his heavy wooden camera. Bussell also had a chaise longue by the side of the studio, which was put into use as a prop for Marie. The session started; I did not know if I should close my eyes as Marie dropped her dressing gown. She gestured that I should keep my eyes open, so I did. I gazed at her unrobed. She had a magnificent body for a woman almost forty. What more can I say? I felt at times that I was in a dream as she put on more provocative poses as the session rolled on. Unclothed, she was even more alive than clothed.

Finally, the session came to an end. I noticed that even Mr Bussell was sweating but then blaming the heat from the studio lights; Marie was unfazed. At the end, she simply stepped to one side, put on her dressing gown, and walked back towards the dressing room. She looked back at me.

'There you are William. Something to remind you of me, while you are away.' I could think of no answer. Mr Bussell was clearly a little shocked but taking it all in his stride. This was after all his business, and those photographs were money in the bank to him.

I was ushered by Mr Bussell back to the front office where he reiterated his desire that this matter should remain confidential and worked out the bill for the pictures taken. They would take a few hours to develop so I paid the requisite deposit and arranged to come back at five o'clock with the full payment and collect the photographs. By the time this transaction was finished, Marie reappeared. She was back in her full silk dress and bodice. Smiling, she took my arm and with a thank you to Mr Bussell, walked me out into the street.

I could still feel the heat of the blush on my cheeks, as we stood together outside the studio. I was totally flummoxed by the turn of events. She seemed happier than I had ever seen her and there was real joy in her voice as she spoke.

'That was nice. It is so long since I have seen a man admire my body – perhaps even desire me. It has been so lonely these last few years.' She gently tapped my crotch. 'I think you may feel the same, no?'

I could hardly contain myself.

'Marie, I have strong feelings for you. I think you know that.' She smiled ever more broadly. 'Good, then let us go to your hotel now.' At that she almost skipped off down the road. I could not believe my luck. I gratefully agreed to her suggestion and a few minutes later I had secreted her into my bedroom at the Eagle.

I will not go into any detail about my liaison with Marie, suffice to say that I now understood why a man who could have had any woman – Louis Napoleon – chose her. Even more glorious than our conjunction was the look in her eyes. The ever-present heartache and pain at the loss of her son had momentarily melted away and she seemed younger and happier than ever before.

Finally, around four o'clock it was time for her to leave. I helped her dress, which in itself seemed a privilege, and we left the Eagle as a couple. Smiling and laughing we walked back up the high street to the station, every time we had to cross a road Marie skipped around the horse's dung, which littered the street, like it was a new game for a child. Obviously if anyone saw us, that might be unhelpful, but we both did not seem to care today. Finally, we reached the station and I saw her on to the London-bound platform. We smiled and chatted then the train arrived out of the tunnel and it was time to say goodbye. I gently took her hand, kissed her fingers, and helped her up the step into the carriage. She blew a kiss and then was gone. I watched the train disappear into the distance. I cannot tell a lie, I was elated. I had experienced a dream come true. Now it was up to me to get to work. If I failed to get her son back that would be it, and I wanted so much more.

I set off back towards Harmer Street to see Mr Bussell. On the way, I went back to the Eagle to collect a package from my bedroom.

TWENTY-THREE

Mr Bussell

I TOOK THE WATCH OUT of my top pocket, flipped open the lid, and noted the time; five o'clock precisely. Having replaced the timepiece, I entered the front door of Mr Bussell's studio. He was there behind the counter and seemed pleased to see me.

'Mr Reeves, so good of you to arrive on time. So many people turn up early and must wait. Your prints are ready and should be dry enough now. Can I suggest some suitable frames for the ones you prefer?'

I eyed him up. He was a nasty piece of work. There was no doubt of that. Behind this very ornate, respectable shop front, all hell must have occurred in his studio over the years.

'Thank you Mr Bussell, I think I'll just take the prints as they are.'

He smiled. 'Of course; I'll fetch them now.' He disappeared into the backroom and emerged seconds later with them. He seemed a little more cautious now.

'Perhaps we should go into the backroom to view these, sir,' he said. I concurred and followed him through to a quiet room away from the public counter. He laid out the photographs of Marie on a table in front of us. In total there were six prints. Even in black and white the beauty and sensuality of that woman shone through. I hated that Bussell could see her in that state, but knew revenge is a dish best served cold.

'Thank you Mr Bussell; I will take them all. You have done a fine job.'

He smiled again more broadly. 'My pleasure Mr Reeves, and I must say you have an exceptionally beautiful wife. Now I will put the prints into a folder and then inside this envelope. You appreciate we must be discreet about these matters?' I nodded in affirmation. Bussell had clearly been more than happy to take the pictures and now would receive a good payment for his trouble. With the pictures in a discreet package we went back to the front desk where he rang up the cost on his till. I paid but then shared my thoughts with him.

'Mr Bussell, I must insist that no further copies of these pictures are made. They are for my benefit only, you understand?'

He was now a picture of contriteness. 'Absolutely Mr Reeves, this studio prides itself on total confidentiality. These are the only prints which will ever be made of today's session.' I looked him square in the eye and brought out the package I had stolen from Bennett's office. In it were the photographs of naked boys.

'So, Mr Bussell, how did I acquire these prints, which I believe were taken here by your good self?'

Bussell looked aghast. He quickly ushered me back into the backroom and stood sweating slightly, his face turning paler by the second.

'Mr Reeves I don't know where you got such filth, but I can assure you that they are not from this studio.'

I knew he did not have a leg to stand on, so continued, 'I bought these prints from Mr John Bennett, the shipping agent, he sold them to me in the King's Arms and was happy to admit that they had been taken in this studio.'

The colour drained from Bussell's face. 'This is slander, I would never allow such a thing to happen in my studio.' He looked almost about to faint.

I decided to let him off the hook, for now. 'Very well, Mr Bussell. I am aware that if these pictures got into the hands of the constabulary, your business and probably your freedom would be at an end. So, we will make a deal. You never, ever, release pictures of my wife. You must now destroy the plates, and I will keep this information quiet.'

He stuttered but was clearly pleased by my offer. 'Of course, Mr Reeves. I will destroy the plates now.' We went into his darkroom and he tipped some plates of glass negatives into an acid bath. 'There you are Mr Reeves, everything from today's session is destroyed apart from what you have.'

I looked him in the eye.

'I hope so Mr Bussell, because if any photographs of my wife leak out from this studio I will personally put your face into that acid bath. We understand each other?'

'Yes, absolutely sir.'

I smiled. 'Then I bid you good day.'

I walked out of the darkroom through the shop and out into the street. Now it would be a waiting game.

TWENTY-FOUR

On the Train

I WENT BACK TO THE Eagle and sat beside the window, so I was able to easily see everything going on down the street, including the brewery entrance. I did not have long to wait. Within minutes a red-faced Mr Bussell strode down the street, clearly in a rage. He entered the brewery works at a furious pace. I knew now that Bennett was getting a piece of his mind in no uncertain terms. Ten minutes later, Bussell emerged. Still red-faced and looking over his shoulder as he walked into the street. He then quickly disappeared, presumably going back to his studio.

I quickly put together a bag containing notepad and binoculars, whilst keeping my other eye on the street. Sure enough, within minutes Bennett appeared. He looked furtively around, then he quickly, or as fast as any man who uses a stick can, scurried off towards the high street. I was out of the Eagle in seconds. Just in time to see Bennett turning right on West Street onto the high street. He was walking uphill towards the town centre. I followed at a distance.

He carried on past the shops and pubs, which edged the street. I had by now guessed his destination. As I expected, he reached the rail station and disappeared into the ticket office. I followed and could see him now, standing on the eastbound platform. I decided to follow my hunch, which was that he was going to see Lynch at his boat, moored on the Medway near Strood. I surreptitiously bought a ticket for Strood and kept to the shadows. When the eastbound train arrived, Bennett was on it straight away, ignoring any attempt to help ladies on first. I waited till the door had banged shut then quickly got into the carriage behind just as the train was leaving the station.

It was now just past six o'clock so the compartment I was in only had suited gentlemen with bowler hats on board, presumably coming home from their desk jobs in the City. I sat down by the window and watched the scenery as the train moved forward through the cutting under the streets of Gravesend. The light came and went as roads overhead crossed the trainline. Then we were out into more open country, I could see the open marshes leading north to the Thames from my window. The other passengers seemed to have no interest in me, which suited me fine. Then we went into a long tunnel. The smoke from the train engine could now be smelt quite strongly; I had opened the carriage window and was not going to shut it till I had caught sight of my prey, much to the annoyance of the other passengers. Finally, we emerged from the tunnel and I could see Strood station ahead. The train slowed, then finally came to a standstill on the platform. I sneaked a look out; yes, there was John Bennett, with his characteristic limp and walking stick, disembarking. I waited until the train was ready to leave then jumped off, much to the annoyance of the station master who clearly prided himself on passenger safety. By now Bennett had left the station so I was able to follow on at a discreet distance. For a man with a walking stick he made great pace. Leaving the station, I could see him heading down the street towards the River Medway. I kept back. Luckily, there were a few other souls going my way, so I was not too noticeable, even if Bennett had turned around.

At the bottom of the street he turned left. I noted the name of the street on a road sign – Canal Street. I paused awhile on the corner to get my bearings. I was virtually on the riverside, surrounded by wharves and businesses connected to the shipping industry. Straight ahead was the Medway itself, and to my right, perhaps a mile distant, was the majestic Rochester Bridge. I looked left along the waterfront and there I saw what I had been half expecting. It was the *Spirit of Rochester*, about half a mile distant, berthed by the riverside at what looked like a shipyard.

Between the shipyard and myself was the remaining section of Canal Street and a riverside inn, the Frying Pan, which faced out over the river. At the end of Canal Street was a canal lock, with a narrow path over it leading to a coal yard and cement works. I could see to my left the massive black heaps of coal stored alongside the quay. Beyond that was a cement factory, with its grey and white dust covering everything close to it. Then there was just open foreshore, with flat marshy land behind it, until you reached the shipyard and the *Spirit*.

After Bennett had crossed the lock gate and disappeared into the alleyway that went through the cement works, I walked up Canal Street as far as the inn. It was a place with windows overlooking the river. Guessing that I would be very exposed if I took the foreshore path to the shipyard, I decided to take sanctuary there.

I walked in; it was a friendly enough place, so I bought a beer and settled myself down by the window. I was soon able to see Bennett's hurrying figure emerge from behind the cement works. Within a minute he was walking the gangplank onto the *Spirit*. My hunch had been correct – he was seeking an emergency meeting with Lynch.

It was now a waiting game. To appear less conspicuous, I got out my notebook and pen and started sketching the riverfront. That way, my staring out of the window would not look that odd. Though the pub was full of working men and was loud at times, they did not bother me. Nevertheless, it was difficult to kill the time without drawing attention to myself. I also had to be careful not to drink too much too soon. I might need a clear head later.

On my second pint the landlord, a well-rounded, middle-aged man with a large purple nose, wandered over to me and spoke warmly. 'The river's beautiful, ain't it sir? Half the people in this beer house don't notice it, but I do.'

I smiled and replied, 'Thank you for that, it restores my faith in human nature. My name's William by the way.'

We shook hands. 'I'm Roy Strong, been the publican here for twenty years. We don't often get artists here, occasionally people come to draw the Rochester Bridge, but not that often.'

The conversation was cut short by some locals clearly wanting service. He went off to see to them while I resumed my seat by the window. It was close to midsummer, so the light was still fine. I sat there for almost two hours. Then finally I saw him, Bennett was leaving the ship and heading back. I bade farewell to Roy and set off down Canal Street to the lock gate. I could see now more detail of the wharves and docks. The lock led to a large basin surrounded by coal yards. A sign proclaimed that this was the coal depot for the South Eastern Rail Company, and I could see beyond the stacks of coal the numerous branch lines joining onto the main Strood to Gravesend Railway. The tide was low, no boats were entering the lock at this time, so the narrow pathway across the lock gates was open for pedestrians.

I secreted myself behind a nearby wall and stared at the lock gate, and alleyway beyond that led to it. I did not have to wait long. Bennett was coming. Scurrying along the alleyway, oblivious to all around him. He reached the lock and slowed at this point as the walkway was narrow and being timber, might be slippery. At this point I darted out from behind the wall. He carried on a few steps before he realised the man in front of him was me. I was the man from Gravesend who asked awkward questions. I stood at one end of the lock gates. He stood at the other end. The passageway was only perhaps thirty inches wide with a steep drop to the canal below us. He glared at me.

'What do you want? Out of my way,' he spat.

'Well Mr Bennett, fancy meeting you here, just after another meeting with your friend Captain Lynch, I presume?'

He stared back.

'What is it to you? Out of my way.'

I stood firm. 'Not till you tell me the whereabouts of Pierre Le Beau.'

He gulped a little at this point; there was fear in his eyes but also grim determination, he was not going to be easily beaten.

'Never heard of him.'

I stood stock still, blocking his path.

'Oh, I think you have. It is the French boy you arranged with Lynch to bring from Rouen to London. But he never made it there. He was taken ashore in Gravesend. Where is he now? Hidden no doubt. I want to know where?'

At this point all pretence was forgotten. He moved towards me and clutching the body of his walking stick, he drew out a sword that had been concealed within it. It was about two feet long and narrow with a vicious-looking tip. Before I had a chance to think of another plan of action, he was at me. He thrust with the sword, aiming at my body. Instinctively I managed to protect my chest by holding my hand across my heart. The sword tip plunged into my wrist, drawing blood. The shock of this made me fall to my knees. He brought the sword out and made ready to thrust it again. There was murder in his eyes. At that moment, a man nearby shouted out, 'What's going on?'

Bennett was literally put off his stroke; he quickly put his sword back into the swordstick and jumped over my semi-prostate figure. He then scurried off down Canal Street. I was still in a state of shock. While the pain was bearable, the blood loss was worrying. I was lucky that within seconds a man arrived – followed by another. I did not know if they were lockkeepers, or just workers passing by, but they probably saved me. The pair dragged me off the lock gate, then lifted me to my feet. With both men holding me up from under my arms, they helped me stumble into the Frying Pan, which was the nearest building. Roy was still there, and seeing my distress, immediately came out from behind the bar. I was sat down, and he called for his wife, who swiftly applied a makeshift tourniquet to stop the blood loss in my arm. I was laid down on one of the benches and a doctor was called. One arrived shortly and quickly stitched up the wound. A member of the Kent constabulary also arrived, but I lied and said that I had been attacked by persons unknown. I was now alright really, the blood loss had stopped and so had the shock of the event. Though I felt a little silly that I had not recognised Bennett's walking stick as a swordstick.

I stayed that night at the Frying Pan, as luckily they had a spare bedroom. I slept fitfully; the pain from my arm was a problem and I distinctly remember being awake at 3 a.m., awoken I presume by the throbbing pain. My thoughts turned to Marie, alone in her bed at Chislehurst and I was warmed by the memories of yesterday. I dozed off again and awoke at eight.

I was immeasurably grateful to Roy and his wife and was happy to pay for the room, and the doctor's bill. My arm was now in a sling. Roy showed me one more act of kindness by persuading the brewer's drayman to give me a lift back to Strood station. The kindness of strangers.

I caught the train back to Gravesend. It was now 10 a.m. I walked slowly back to the Eagle; it had been a long night.

TWENTY-FIVE

Back to Chislehurst

MARIE HAD ARRIVED BACK AT Chislehurst at seven o'clock the preceding evening, having been picked up from Sidcup station by one of Napoleon's staff. Back at the house the atmosphere seemed strange. Louis had taken to his bed with another round of his interminable illnesses, mostly painful kidney stones, and it appeared that Antonia was now in charge of his comfort. Marie could not really care less. She had had enough of this dreadful fiasco of living with an emperor with no empire. She was an exile in a foreign land without any real position at the Emperor's court.

The only thing that made her feel good about herself was William. With him, for the first time in years, she felt like someone desirable, not just a chattel to be used on demand. But her daydreaming made no difference to her day-to-day life, and that night, as always, she went to bed alone.

Her sleep was broken in the middle of the night. She awoke with a start. She could hear Toulouse outside the front door talking loudly to somebody. Marie leapt out of bed and went to the window. Clearly something had occurred. She could hear his voice saying, 'So you didn't catch sight of the horseman?'

The other man replied, 'No sir, he just dropped this by the gates and rode off. He was too fast for us.'

Toulouse grunted. 'Very well, get back to your post.' At that he came back into the house and disappeared off to his bedroom.

Was this another letter from the kidnappers, another ransom demand? Marie glanced at the clock in her bedroom; it was three o'clock. In normal circumstances she would have banged on his bedroom door and demanded to see the letter, but the atmosphere at the house was so toxic now, she hesitated. Matthew hated her, if she demanded to see the letter he might refuse outright. The protocol was that Louis Napoleon would see it first if it were addressed to him. Marie closed the bedroom door and went back to her bed. She would have to wait until morning, then things would become clearer.

She woke at seven and went down to the servants' quarters kitchen to see what needed to be done. Matthew Toulouse was already there. He was a bald man with a silly pointed moustache, much as the Emperor had in past years. He was about forty years of age. He was a creep of the first order, always politicking and feeding poisonous rumours to Louis Napoleon.

'Good morning Marie, so good for you to condescend to spend some time with us, fulfilling your duties to the house.' Marie felt belittled but stood her ground.

'Louis gave me express permission to go to Gravesend to see what I could find out about my missing son. You know that.'

He smiled thinly. 'Indeed, finding your missing son. That seems to have somewhat taken over your life. Luckily for us, Antonia is perfectly capable of fulfilling all your roles and will wake and breakfast our Emperor today.'

'I am perfectly willing and capable of providing for all of his needs.'

Toulouse twiddled his moustache. 'Indeed, I'm sure you are. However, things are changing. Perhaps we need to discuss your position further? If you could meet me in the drawing room at 10 a.m., we can talk through things in private.' He smiled again, even his smile seemed like a snake's hiss.

'Very well, I will meet you then. Before that can I enquire about a letter delivered here last night, about three o'clock, by a horse rider?'

His smile had now disappeared. 'A letter addressed to the Emperor was delivered. I will be discussing its contents with Louis later this morning before I meet you. Now can I get on with business?' It was clearly the end of the discussion. Marie nodded and went back to her room.

At 10 a.m. prompt Marie took her seat in the drawing room. She was alone in the fine room with its tapestry-style wallpaper and velvet curtains. Ten minutes later Matthew Toulouse appeared. He looked as pretentious and pompous as Marie had ever seen him. He closed the door behind him. Marie stood up and curtseyed. Matthew nodded and bade her to sit down. He fiddled with his moustache and smoothed down his suit before speaking.

'Marie, I have been speaking to Louis about your predicament. We are both obviously saddened by the kidnap of little Pierre but have some concerns that this matter is overwhelming your ability to do your duties here at the house.' Marie was stunned.

'Let me speak to Louis, he will understand if I explain things to him.'

Matthew sighed. 'I'm afraid it has gone beyond that. I believe that you would benefit from returning to Paris, obviously with a new identity. That way you could start a new, and better, life for yourself.' Marie could not believe her ears; she felt her whole world crumbling before her.

She tried to interrupt but to no avail.

'Of course, you would be paid a small allowance to help you start your new life.'

Her shock now turned to anger. 'But Pierre is the son of the Emperor. All my efforts to find him are for Louis as well.'

Matthew's smile was almost sickening.

'I am sorry, but the Emperor is not a well man, also he is not convinced that Pierre is his child, so his interest in this matter is purely academic.'

Marie was now crestfallen; this was a hammer blow. She fought back as best she could.

'I demand to see Louis. I demand it.'

Matthew was unmoved and becoming smugger by the minute. 'I am afraid that is totally impossible. He is going into one of London's finest hospitals, later today, to have gallstones removed. He is not fit enough to see you. The decision is made. However, as a sign of my compassion for your predicament, we will allow you to remain at the house until you can settle your affairs here. That time you should remain in your bedroom. Your meals will be left outside the door, as will a fresh chamber pot.'

This was it then, the final humiliation. She knew Toulouse must not destroy her. Marie recovered her composure.

'That horse rider in the night, did he bring another ransom demand? Is that what has upset Louis?'

Matthew spoke slowly. 'The contents of the letter are private, but I intend to convey them to the relevant authority, who I believe is Lieutenant-Colonel Gordon, based at Gravesend.'

Marie was unhappy at Matthew even knowing this. 'How do you know Gordon is involved?'

He smiled thinly. 'I have sources in Gravesend. I also believe you have. In fact, rumours have reached my ears that you have been indiscreet, with some tuppenny ha'penny journalist, by the name of William Reeves.' Marie felt denuded by this. 'Of course, I have not given Louis all the details, as he is a sick man and has always held you in high regard. Your fealty to him has always been something he valued highly, so I have not mentioned this matter. Yet. I hope you appreciate my discretion in this matter.'

Marie was broken by this; her fifteen-year relationship with Napoleon, albeit for the last few years just a friendship, was the reason she had followed him into exile in London.

'I think that brings our little conversation to an end Marie. Now if you could return to your room I can continue with business.'

Marie stood up as best she could, her legs had turned to jelly but she managed a cursory curtsey. Toulouse had not heard the last of this. When Louis was well enough she would get things changed, but for now she had to accept her fate. She stood tall, then walked out of the room and back up the stairs to her lonely bedroom. It felt as if her life were over, but she would never let Toulouse think that she was weak or broken.

PART 3

Dark places for dark deeds

TWENTY-SIX

The Fort

I HAD SOME CONCERNS ABOUT the sword wound. It was hurting like hell and badly bruised. I was also beginning to feel feverish which might have been a reaction to the wound or sign of an infection. I was too unwell to sleep so around noon decided to go and see the medical officer at the fort.

My face was well-known there now, and I was able to speak to the medical officer. He looked at my wound with some concern but seemed to conclude it was not infected. The fever was probably just a reaction to the shock and pain.

Happy with this diagnosis I wondered off from his room and out into the small parade ground at the centre of the fort.

The sun was shining, and I took advantage of this to try and relax and let nature do the healing. Within a few minutes Asif appeared. He had been doing some construction work on the ramparts and was now taking his lunchbreak. He was clearly pleased to see me.

'Mr Reeves, you look unwell. What is the matter with your arm?'

I tried to raise a brave smile. 'Just a flesh wound. Had a fallout with John Bennett, and he got the knife in first.'

Asif sat down beside me. 'That John Bennett is an evil man sir, but we will get revenge on him.'

I mopped my brow. 'I hope so Asif, I really do.'

We sat there for a while saying nothing, so I opened the conversation.

'How is it going here at the fort? I can see they have found plenty of work for you.'

'Very good sir, I am very happy here.' He smiled.

'Good, you realise that this is only a temporary arrangement. We will have to find you a new ship at some point.'

He looked saddened by this but as always was a realist. 'Yes, I know that as well, but the people here in Gravesend have been good to me.'

I nodded. 'Tell me something of yourself Asif. How did you become a sailor – how did it start?'

He answered me openly as always. 'I was in my hometown looking for work, things were difficult in Zanzibar. My family had a good business importing and exporting textiles. I traded with many people and learnt to speak good English. But other people were jealous of us, we were doing too well. There was a business dispute and they burnt down our house. We had little money put by so could not start all over again. So, I looked for a new position. Times were hard, not enough work, not enough money to buy food. I heard that ships were calling at the harbour looking for crew. So, I went there. Mr Lynch's ship was sailing back from Calicut with a cargo of spice and ivory. It stopped at Zanzibar and I was lucky enough to be taken on as a hand. The boat was bound for London, but I knew it would return later for another load of spices. So, one day I would return to my homeland.'

I could feel there was a story in this, so pressed on.

'So, you got a position on the boat sailing to England. What was it like working for Lynch?'

Asif screwed up his face. 'It was not that good. Hard work, tough discipline, many unhappy crewmen. I can give you an example of what it was like, and the kind of man that Captain Lynch is. We had a young English crew member, a junior officer. I think his name was Tom Carter. He was ill with malaria. No sooner had we left Zanzibar than he was sent to the sick quarters. The boat sailed down the east coast of Africa and I thought we would make many stops for fresh provisions, but that did not happen. I had heard that the other officers were urging Captain Lynch to stop at Cape Town, to get fresh food and water, and to take Mr Carter ashore to a hospital, but Lynch would not stop. Some people say he had guaranteed getting his load of spices back to London by a certain date. Others think he had a bet on with another captain that the *Spirit* could outrun him and reach England first. So, we sailed straight past Cape Town and did not stop again till we reached Freetown, in West Africa. By now Mr Carter was dying. He died while we were moored off that town. Mr Lynch seemed unconcerned. Buried the body at sea. Then reloaded the boat as soon as possible and raced up the African coast. He wouldn't stop till we got to England.' Asif sat back; his story told. I could not believe my ears. The junior officer, Tom Carter, could that be Jack Carter's son? And if so, did Jack know the whole story, or did Lynch tell him that he fell sick while at Freetown? I looked at Asif; this man was my saviour.

'Thanks for that Asif, it tells me a lot about Lynch's character. When you got to England what happened? Was there any trouble over Tom Carter's death?'

Asif shrugged. 'We stopped for an hour or so at Gravesend for Customs. I think his death was reported but we were told never to talk about it, to leave all that to the captain.'

Now why didn't that surprise me?

At that moment I noticed Asif's gang getting back to work. 'I think your tea break is up now, but thanks for that. That information could be more useful than you think.' Asif went back to his duties and I sat and pondered. Had Lynch told the authorities the full story? No, he would have lied through his teeth to make sure there were no repercussions.

If I were able to tell Carter the unvarnished truth, could I get him on board? Would he open up about Lynch and maybe give some clues as to the location of Pierre? Perhaps, but it was not guaranteed. I was unsure of my next move.

At that moment, the decision was made for me; a subaltern came out of the fort offices and spoke to me.

'Mr Reeves, Gordon would like to see you immediately.'

I rose to my feet, smiling. 'Good.' I was pleased to be seeing Gordon. That way I could update him on what had occurred and pick his brain as to my next move. I knocked on his office door.

'Come in Reeves.'

The familiar sound of Gordon's voice came back, but this time there was something less friendly in its tone. When I entered the office, I could see him at his desk, but opposite him was a tall, balding man with a sharp, greased moustache, who I had never seen before. Gordon spoke first.

'Thanks for coming Reeves. I see you have been in the wars?'

'Just a silly accident, no permanent damage.'

'Let me introduce my guest. Mr Matthew Toulouse, the Chief of Staff to Emperor Louis Napoleon.'

The Frenchman rose to his feet and put an outstretched hand to me. We shook hands; his handshake was as oily as his thinning hair!

'Pleased to meet you,' I said.

'The pleasure is all mine,' he replied. Gordon bade us to sit down then immediately made clear the nature of the meeting.

'Now obviously relations with our neighbours across the channel are always sensitive, so I would be grateful, Reeves, if you could keep quiet about this meeting.'

I nodded. 'Of course.'

Gordon continued. 'Very well, now Mr Toulouse has some information regarding the kidnap of Pierre Le Beau. He has been kind enough to allow me access to a letter, dropped off last night at the Emperor's home in Chislehurst, stating the terms of Pierre's release. He is happy for us to have this correspondence, and to do what we will with it. Is that correct Mr Toulouse?' The Frenchman twiddled the ends of his moustache.

'Indeed, it is. Let me firstly update you on what has occurred. A letter was left on the ground beside the gates leading to the Emperor's house, at about three o'clock this morning. Inside the envelope was a ransom demand. The horse rider who delivered the letter could not be apprehended. At first light I showed the delivered papers to Louis Napoleon himself, who I might add is in poor health now. He considered the contents of the letter carefully and asked me to see you, as we know there has been some activity in relation to the investigation of the boy's disappearance, here in Gravesend.' He paused and choosing his words carefully, continued, 'To put it simply, the Emperor is now very tired of this whole affair. He is most sensitive to his relationship with Great Britain and your gracious Queen Victoria. He also realises that we are guests in your country and therefore does not want to cause upset. So, he has decided that the issue of Pierre's disappearance is to be pursued no longer. No ransom will be paid and the Empresses former lady-in-waiting, and mother of the boy, Marie-Anne, will not be travelling to Gravesend again.' He paused and looked over to me, then continued, 'As her presence appears to be a distraction.'

Toulouse looked long and hard at me. I knew at that moment that he knew, or guessed, what had occurred. I had to speak.

'My understanding is that Marie was very anxious to find Pierre and would do anything to achieve that aim.'

Toulouse gave a thin smile. 'Indeed, but her first duty is to the Emperor, so she will stay at the house in Chislehurst tending to his needs. As I say, you are free to do what you wish, but in reality we must sadly admit that Pierre is now a lost cause. That gives me great sadness but there is no further action we can take to find him. The Emperor will not be funding your role as an investigator Mr Reeves, neither will we pay any ransom to get the boy back.'

He seemed to have said his piece. I was struggling to find what to say. It appeared they were willing to forget Pierre and write him off altogether. I then found the courage to speak from my heart.

'You cannot do that. I have spoken to Marie and know of her total dedication to finding her son. She will be heartbroken by this.' Toulouse was clearly not one for backing off.

'My understanding, from sources here in the town, is that perhaps you have got too close to Marie. No? Perhaps that, what shall we call it, your friendship, is clouding your judgement.'

I could feel the blood rushing to my face.

'Marie is a fine woman and I find her love for her son, and determination to find him, a very noble thing.' Toulouse looked at me, then at Gordon.

'Come gentlemen, we are men of the world. Firstly, you must know that there is no proof whatsoever that the boy is the son of our Emperor. Admittedly Marie was a close friend of Louis for over fifteen years, but there is no proof of parentage. The child is a bastard.'

I could barely contain my annoyance and could feel my fingernails pressing into my palms trying to contain my anger.

'What proof do you have of that sir?' I said in as reasoned a tone as I could manage.

Toulouse gave that deep but contemptible smile, as if he were dealing with imbeciles.

'Dear Mr Reeves, I don't think you realise the sort of life we lived in Paris, at the Tuileries. Let me explain. We used to have masked balls where much wine was drunk. The masks allowed us to hide our identity and, shall we say, behave with greater freedom of expression. During the course of the night, women, like Marie, might have had several partners. In fact, I myself may have had conjunction with her.' He was now in full stride. 'It is difficult to remember when so much is drunk, and the women are weak willed,' he smirked.

Gordon was by now red-faced and clearly discomforted by this talk. I was almost incandescent with rage.

Luckily, Gordon spoke first, in clipped tones. 'I think we have heard enough Monsieur Toulouse.'

The Frenchman smiled but continued. 'Of course, the other problem that came from the masked balls was venereal disease. Loose women spreading it to the court.'

I could hold myself back no longer.

'With the greatest respect it is not just women who are the spreaders of such disease.'

Toulouse was now on the back foot. He said the single word. 'Indeed.' An awkward silence filled the room.

Finally, Gordon rose out of his chair. 'I think we have got the picture Mr Toulouse. Now if you can take your leave, I will discuss the contents of the letter with Mr Reeves.'

The Frenchman got out of his seat, clicked his heels, and put out his hand. There were awkward handshakes all round. Gordon clearly sensed the atmosphere and felt obliged to add some small talk.

'Will you be alright finding your way back to Gravesend station?'

Toulouse smiled. 'Of course, and I must commend you on the quality of your railways. In fact, I will mention this at my next meeting with Her Majesty Queen Victoria.'

He clicked his heels again, and then left the office.

Gordon and I looked at each other in silence, waiting for the Frenchman to get well out of earshot. Clearly Toulouse's role had been to both dispose of the ransom note, and to poison any possible relationship between Marie and myself.

Gordon sat back down, and I followed his lead. He spoke first.

'Nasty piece of work. Typical Frenchman. Slimy and underhand.'

I had now calmed down but felt determined to defend Marie's reputation.

'I couldn't agree more, what he insinuated about Marie was both cruel and probably untrue.'

Gordon dipped his head but added some words of caution.

'Indeed, a nasty man, but if you have been indiscreet with Napoleons' lady, you can expect to be the subject of criticism.'

I knew he was right but had no real defence, I had allowed personal interests to get in the way of the investigation. I was also upset about Toulouse's talk of orgies in Paris. With most men I could have had a candid 'heart to heart', but Gordon was such a cold fish. I had no idea if he had any interest in sex, or whether he had even had a woman; certainly, I knew him to be a confirmed bachelor with no obvious female interest in his life. So, I decided to hide my feelings and get back to the business in hand.

'Could you be so kind as to read the contents of the ransom note?' Gordon unfolded the paper in front of him and read slowly. 'The letter is addressed to Louis Napoleon himself and it states the following:

We have the boy Pierre in our custody. We will release him back to you if you comply with the following:
Gold ingots, to the value of ten thousand guineas, to be brought to the following location, and under

these auspices. The gold should be secreted on a cart and transported westbound along the old London road from Gravesend towards Dartford, on Sunday the 1st July, commencing the journey at 8 p.m., precisely. At some point on the journey you will be stopped, and the gold exchanged for the captive. If you agree to these terms please place an advert in the Kent Messenger, this Friday, stating that you have a house for sale in East Street, Gravesend for 300 guineas and giving your address for correspondence as: Fenchurch Street Chartered Surveyors, Leadenhall, City of London.

Gordon looked up from the papers and added a caveat. 'I have already checked and found that no such firm of surveyors exist.' He sat back in his chair. I was both pleased that matters appeared to be coming to a head, and terrified about what action to take.

'Well Reeves, I think that puts the final nail in the coffin. Unless you have ten thousand guineas in your back pocket that is! It also appears that the French court will not pay this ransom or give financial support to your investigation. So, perhaps now is the time to end this whole affair.'

I knew that must not happen, I owed too much to Marie for that. 'No, never, I will go on until Pierre is found, even if it costs me everything... Now let me think about this.' I paused for a moment searching for anything that could salvage the situation, then came out with a suggestion. 'Gold is what they want. They have no morality, no other motive. It is interesting that they want it in the form of ingots. Presumably, it is easier to hide and not as traceable as bank notes. Of course, I cannot afford that, but what if I could fool them? What if I could get some ingots made up from brass? They might look enough like gold bars to get close to the kidnappers, and steal the boy away before they realised the deception?'

Gordon sighed audibly.

'Brass does not look like gold, even an idiot can tell the difference.'

I was not giving up so easily. 'Did you see the time of the exchange proposed? I would not be leaving Gravesend until eight in the evening. With luck it would be past sunset before the transfer took place. In the dark the brass might look close enough to the real thing to fool the perpetrators. It is worth a shot. We've got nothing to lose.'

Gordon clearly was not convinced. 'So, you would go to see these murderers with nothing more than some worthless brass bars on a cart. It's madness.'

'I'll take Asif with me. He is a good man in a crisis. I am willing to try it. Would it be possible for your blacksmith to knock up some fake gold bars for me to use? I know it asking a lot, but the boy's life is at stake here.'

Gordon retorted, 'And your relationship with Napoleon's lady as well, no doubt?'

I could not be stopped now and ignored his comment.

'I'm just asking you this, as a favour. I know what a fine Christian man you are. I know how you hate to see children abused and mistreated. I know you will see it as your Christian duty to support me.'

He looked at me long and hard, then smiled slightly. 'Very well, get some rest today and make sure your arm is on the mend. Come to the fort tomorrow and I will introduce you to our blacksmith and see if it is possible to create fake gold. Getting a cart to carry them on will be no problem, I can provide that. I will leave you to contact the local paper with the house advert. Beyond that I cannot be involved. If it all goes horribly wrong, and it may, it is your responsibility. We understand each other.'

I was relieved. 'Of course. And thank you very much Gordon. This means a lot to me.'

We shook hands and the meeting was concluded.

TWENTY-SEVEN

Into the
Valley of Death

LATER THAT DAY, I PLACED the advert in the *Kent Messenger* and by the following morning felt better. I walked down to the fort and was greeted by Gordon.

'I hope you have slept well?'

I smiled. 'Indeed, and I'm feeling much better.'

'Good, let me take you round the fort before we meet the blacksmith.'

He led on and walked up the steep grass embankment to the fort walls from where we could see up and down the river. 'Modern day forts, Reeves, are entirely different from the old medieval castles. Here it is not about the thickness of the perimeter walls, but the earth banked up against them. That will absorb any shells fired from the river. We have ten rifle muzzled loaded nine-inch guns on the brick emplacements protected by iron, that is why we have a metalworker on site. I cannot tell you the range of the guns, that's an official secret, but I can tell you that working in co-ordination with Tilbury Fort, on the other side of the river, we can cover every inch of the navigable Thames with gunfire at this point. It would be almost impossible for a hostile navy to get through our barrage and reach London.'

He stood back clearly pleased with his works. I could not help but be in awe of what he had achieved. 'Very impressive. You have done a fine job here, Gordon, by the look of it.'

He never took praise well. 'It is what I do Reeves. Odd thing is all these works were commissioned to protect us from the French Navy. Now we are moving heaven and earth to save one of their citizens.' He proffered a tentative smile then put his hands behind his back and led me down to the blacksmith's shop, adjacent to the parade ground.

After some cursory introductions Gordon outlined to the blacksmith, who was a stout fellow – whose name coincidentally was Smith – what was required. Without much ado Smith agreed to his request and set about creating some fool's gold. Our meeting had concluded, and Gordon returned to his office.

I then went in search of Asif. Usually he was very noticeable, being the only lascar who worked at the fort. After some searching I detected some cigar smoke coming from behind a wall. I looked over it and there was Asif on his own, puffing away on a hand-rolled cheroot. He looked at me with fear.

'Please, Mr Reeves do not tell the General about this. Strict man. Too many explosives here, very bad to smoke.'

I smiled. 'It's alright Asif, I think you're safe here.' I breathed in the tobacco smoke. 'I used to smoke myself but gave it up when it started to affect my breathing. Still enjoy the odd cigar though.'

He seemed relieved. 'Thing is Asif I need your help. I am taking a cartload of gold up the London road on Sunday, to exchange it for Pierre. Will you be my second man?'

'I would be most pleased to assist you,' he beamed.

'But I must warn you that this is an extremely dangerous mission, both our lives will be in jeopardy. Do you still want to be part of it?'

'Yes sir, most definitely.'

'Good. Now that cheroot you are smoking has given me an idea. If we can put some fireworks on the cart, hidden away of course, they might come in handy. Any spot of bother and you can light the touch paper with your cheroot and start a small explosion. Might be a useful diversion. I will be bringing my handgun as well, that will be kept out of sight. Do not mention any of this to Gordon. Agreed?'

He was like a kid at his first day at school. 'Yes, sir.'

I reached into my pocket. 'Here is a guinea, go into town and find a shop that sells fireworks. Make sure you get a good mix. The more noise and colour the better.' At that he scuttled off. I was pleased; a plan was coming together. Now roll on Sunday night. We were ready for action. I left the fort and went back to the hotel to rest awhile.

As Sunday evening grew nearer I was besieged by doubts and fear. Should I try and contact Marie to let her know about it? How could we grab Pierre and whisk him away before our enemies discovered the gold bars were just burnished brass? What lay in store for us? Anything could happen between Gravesend and Dartford. Would we be held up by some latter-day Dick Turpin, or taken to some secret location? I really had no idea. The only thing I was sure of was that telling Marie would be a mistake. Raising her hopes might just be a precursor to a crushing disappointment. Better to keep her in the dark. What else had we to go on? The timing was interesting, an 8 p.m. start, so we would be doing much of the journey in twilight. Might it aid our cause if it was dark? Perhaps the gold bars might look more realistic by moonlight, and buy us some precious time?

Should we be equipped with guns? That would be illegal, and in any case I had not fired one since my time in Crimea. However, after my experience at Strood, maybe it was a good idea.

Time moved on towards the Sunday. The advert appeared in the *Kent Messenger*, as requested. All was set.

So, come Sunday evening we took charge of a pair and a sturdy cart, all provided by Gordon. Now it had come to the time for action, I was feeling a cold lump in the pit of my stomach. I turned to my loyal friend Asif.

'You do realise that we may not come out of this alive?'

Asif's face did not flinch. 'I have great faith in you Master Reeves. It is written in the stars that we will succeed. I am sure of that.' At that the conversation was at an end and we set about the business in hand. Both myself and Asif were capable drivers, so as long as the horses behaved, I was confident of making a steady pace.

We found a good place inside the fort – but out of sight, and loaded the gold and fireworks on board, and covered them with heavy-duty canvas. Asif was a godsend; he seemed unperturbed by this whole affair. Perhaps being on board a sailing ship with Lynch as captain, you were used to taking on difficult tasks and risking your life every day?

Certainly, he had become a very trusted companion, clever, resourceful, and utterly loyal.

We set off from the fort through Gravesend, the horses were easy to handle. Asif sat up top beside me. It was another warm, sultry night. We trotted through the quiet Gravesend streets, heading west towards the old London road. It was now 8 p.m. We had no idea if we were being watched; I kept looking up at the lace curtained first-floor windows of the houses we passed, looking for movement from prying eyes, but saw nothing suspicious. In any case we were following instructions and sticking to the agreed timings.

I wanted it to be dark when we met our kidnappers, so I had already decided on a little bit of theatre to buy us time and get us closer to sunset, and the cloak of darkness. Just a few hundred yards along the London road, I stopped the horses quickly and yelled at Asif to look at the wheels. It was pure theatre, but I had no idea if we were being watched, certainly there was no sign of us being followed. Asif took a long look at the wheel axle and then got some tools, a hammer, and pliers, from the toolkit that lived on the back of the cart. He then banged away on the axle for a few minutes on the pretext that there was some misalignment of the wheels. I shouted various words of annoyance to add to this bizarre show. All the while I kept a lookout along the road, there was little traffic – Sunday evening was a quiet time. Finally, with much faux relief, Asif finished his banging about and put the tools away and resumed his seat alongside me. The 'repair' had taken us a good twenty minutes, whether this time would be crucial, I had no idea. We carried on our way.

To our right, looking north, we could see the upcoming port area of Northfleet and to our left the start of the chalk hillsides, which I knew stretched most of the way to Dartford. This had not that long ago been virgin landscape, now it bore the scars of chalk quarrying and the spread of industry.

We kept up an even, slow pace. I felt an awareness of the great history of this Roman road which was the main route from Dover to London. For centuries it had been used by pilgrims going to Canterbury. Some years ago, it had featured in Charles Dickens' *A Tale of Two Cities* – back then it was all about the stagecoaches hammering down the highway on their way to Paris; now the train was king, and the road was quieter. The horses trotted on at an even pace.

We had by now reached Swanscombe, which was still not even halfway to Dartford, and there had been absolutely no sign of anything suspicious. Looking to my right again I could see the River Thames very clearly. It was a fine scene as the sun was setting in the west casting long shadows behind us. Even though it was a busy commercial waterway, the Thames still had a kind of magic and I allowed myself a few moments of relief, just watching the fading sunlight reflect off its meandering course. Then an unexpected sight broke into my reverie. Just off the riverside, moored alongside a jetty and probably a mile distant, was a China clipper. I looked hard, yes, there was no doubt, it was the *Spirit of Rochester*! Clearly the fire damage repairs had been completed, and it was ready to get back to work. I pointed her out to Asif. He looked backed excitedly. There was no doubt it was his ship. Was this some bizarre coincidence, or was it in some way involved in this ransom demand? Surely it was just too unlikely. I turned to Asif.

'What do you think? Why is it moored over there?'

He shook his head. Thoughts were already rattling around in my mind.

'You know what I think – it's moored up there waiting for a cargo of chalk or flint from the workings near here. Could be taking them anywhere. Probably flint going up to Liverpool, then on to the potteries by canal.'

Asif nodded. We rode on.

It was now about nine thirty and dusk was gathering. To our left we could see the rising hillsides, just shapes now in the twilight, and the white of the exposed chalk workings, slightly reddened by the last rays of sunlight, standing out against the darkening sky.

Our pair were now struggling slightly as we pushed on up an incline in the road. This caused us to slow slightly, and the horses' strides shortened. It looked as if the incline was caused by a small railway, probably a tramway, going under the main London road. This area was full of tramways, which ran the excavated chalk and flint down to the river jetties. At its top was a gentle humpback bridge. Thinking nothing of this, I reached down for my pocket watch to check the time. It was nine thirty-five precisely.

Just then, my eyes were suddenly aware of movement. Two mounted horsemen had emerged out of the hedgerow beside the road and reined their mounts to block our path. I had no choice but to bring our horses to a grinding halt. The two men were mounted on rough-looking steeds, probably gypsy horses. They had working men's caps on and their faces were masked, they were both dressed in dirty working clothes with heavy boots. Both had rifles, which were pointed directly at us. One shouted 'Stop.' Followed by 'This way.' He gestured towards a narrow side road which branched off the carriageway. I put my hand up to show my agreement with this and then manoeuvred the carriage down into the side road, which was in fact little more than a bumpy earthen track. I had to move gingerly at first, as the carriage gradually descended down to the level of the railway line that came under London road. The two men followed at a distance with their rifles still pointed at us. At the bottom of the slope the land flattened out somewhat and I noted the tramway was on a slight incline climbing away from the road, and the river beyond, towards more chalk works. The track then followed alongside the railway, which was a narrow-gauge affair. Usually this meant two railway lines running side by side, probably run on a drum pulley system with no engine – just the weight of the loads taking the bogies downhill to the river being used to drag the empty bogies back up the hill.

I looked at Asif; he was still calm, unlike myself. This was getting scary. It was also making sense, any load from the chalk pit could be run down to a ship moored on the jetty, and what better ship for these thugs than the *Spirit*, which was berthed there. Things were becoming clearer. It was not just coincidence that Lynch's boat was here, it had work to do, ferrying the gold bars away!

The two horsemen kept their distance. So, it felt like we were on our own. I looked around. It was past sunset now, and the light was going. We were in a massive chalk pit. A man-made valley. I remembered from Crimea the infamous Charge of the Light Brigade. 'Into the valley of death'. Could this be our valley of death, our fate now?

The chalk escarpments rose steeply to both sides of the tramway. They were sheer cliffs of chalk. I remembered reading somewhere that miners would hang on the cliffsides, and hit the chalk with picks and shovels, then watch the chalk drop straight into the open trucks on the tramway below – a precarious living.

Our horse and cart carried on along the track, it was slightly uphill, and worse, very poorly laid with innumerable bumps and hollows to negotiate. Finally, in the dusky light ahead, we could see a group of open wagons, or bogies, parked up on the tramway. So presumably this was the end of the line. I counted them, there were six in all. Just visible, beyond the line of bogies, was a tunnel into which the tramway had been laid, probably going on to another pit. Standing at the entrance to the tunnel were two figures silhouetted in the half light. The men were both stoutly built with one a little taller than the other. Beyond that there was little clue as to their identity, as both had their faces covered by scarves. We could both sense that this was our destiny. The waiting was over.

I slowly brought the wagon to a halt about ten yards in front of them, making sure that the horses and cart were facing directly onto the tunnel entrance. Also, Asif without hesitation lit up a cheroot and puffed away.

I noted that the two men were rough-looking, and both holding rifles, which were pointed directly at us. I glanced up at the cliffside, where I could see small beacons lit up. There were some more men above us, standing on the cliffs, also presumably with guns pointing at us. This was not looking good.

The taller of the men spoke first.

'Have you got the gold?'

I answered in the affirmative, he continued.

'Take it off the cart and carry it over to the open wagon. Do it slowly.'

Following instructions to the letter, we got down off the carriage. Such was the tension; I had put both my hands above my head in a sign of surrender. The man spoke again, more brusquely.

'Get on with it.'

I walked to the back of the cart, pulled back the canvas and picked up one of the gold bars, Asif did likewise. We then carried the bars to the wagons. For some reason I decided that the first wagon was the right place to put them. This being at the front, and lowest point, of the six coupled bogies. This would be the first to leave if the wagons headed towards the riverside. We then repeated the process several times, so had all the bars deposited as requested in the instructions. The second masked man came over to the wagon and luckily – barely glancing at the gold – covered it with flints. All the time the guns remained pointed at us. I was now standing by the tramway; I looked at the main man.

'That is it then, gold bars to the value of ten thousand guineas. We have kept our side of the bargain. Now where is the boy, Pierre?'

The man laughed.

'Idiots, there is no boy. There is nothing for you here.'

At that, the second man picked up a large pickaxe handle that had been resting against the side of the tunnel. I noted that the handle had massive six-inch nails at its working end. The main man spoke tersely but coldly to him.

'Finish the job.'

At that the man raised the handle above his head and moved in my direction. I pulled my revolver from its holster, which was secreted under my clothes. 'Stop right there!' I shouted. He paused.

Asif seemed to read my mind and quietly took his cheroot from his mouth and touched its flaming end onto the fuse. This movement seemed unnoticed by our enemies. I was expecting to be shot, there and then. They had men in front of us, above us and behind us. But no, there was some hesitation. Of course! They did not want the sound of gunshots! The sound would reverberate around this valley, carry too far, and raise suspicions. They wanted to kill us quietly. For a few moments we were all frozen. The main man had to make a decision – could he risk the sound of gunfire? Then the decision was made for him. All hell broke loose! The fireworks on the cart exploded with some force. Rockets whizzed over our heads, jumping jacks and roman candles were going off in all directions. Our horses bolted, and, as I had hoped, reared up, then galloped straight ahead towards the men in the tunnel. The two horsemen, who had been loitering behind us, fared no better. One of the horses bolted, throwing the rider off. The other horse was inconsolable and galloped around in circles with the rider hanging on for dear life. Despite this confusion, I could sense we were still vulnerable to an onslaught of bullets from the gunmen on the cliffs above, so grabbed Asif and ran swiftly to the tramway. We took shelter behind the first iron wagon, which had the fool's gold in it. We were just in time. Bullets thudded into the ground around us and pinged against the iron of the bogie above our heads, too close for comfort. The tall man seemed to be out of it, having been knocked over by the maddened horses, and was lying on the ground clearly in pain. Despite this, we were still just sitting ducks.

Trapped in a quarry with who knows how many gunmen above us.

An idea came to me; what if the wagons were just held by brakes? If I could release them then the bogies might roll of their own accord. I could see an iron handle which seemed connected to the bogie's axle. I grabbed it and wrenched it open. For a few seconds nothing changed then, almost imperceptibly, our wagon started to move away from the others. We grabbed on to the side holding on by our fingertips. Bullets rained down. Then the wagon picked up speed. We were clinging on for grim death, but we were moving out of the gunshot range of the killers above us.

With every yard we went the gunmen's bullets were less accurate in the gathering darkness. Soon we were out of range of the guns. The bogie by now was careering downhill. We had no way of controlling it, or regulating its speed, without braking. As it gathered pace, we both managed to somehow clamber on top of it and lie on the flint load. We had somehow escaped with our lives but had not seen any sign of Pierre. So, the whole escapade had been a failure. For the time being our priority was just self-preservation.

I was in two minds as to what to do next, should we stay on the wagon till it careered into the sleepers at the jetty? Or get off as soon as possible? We both seemed to have the same answer, to get out with our skins still intact. I could see us now approaching the short tunnel that went under the London road. I reached down and with my boot, feathered the brake. Slowly, imperceptibly, we started to slow. I exerted more pressure and we came to a grinding halt. We were now under the bridge. Aware that the two masked horsemen might have recovered their horses and followed us, we slid off the wagon and stealthily climbed out of the tunnel and up the bank onto the main road. We were clearly exposed here, but so would be armed horsemen.

I could now hear the rattling of the bogies below us. Without my restraint, it had gathered speed and was rolling out of the tunnel down towards the river. Presumably, it would not stop until it hit the buffers at the jetty. That would be a nice mess for Lynch to clear up! And they would only worthless bars of brass to show for their intrigue. That would not even pay for the smashed-up wagon and buffers!

I looked up and down the road. Even on a Sunday night there would be some horse and carriages passing this way. It was all quiet. By now dusk had turned to night. I decided on the simplest course of action.

'Asif, let us see if we can retrace our tracks and walk back to Gravesend. If we hear anything on the road then slip off it into the hedgerows and let them pass.'

And that we did. It was probably about three or four miles to Gravesend. Walking briskly, we made it in under an hour. Nobody followed us and we met no passing traffic, which could have provided us with a lift back into town.

We walked on regardless and arrived just before midnight in sleepy Gravesend.

I had some concerns we might be followed so decided to seek sanctuary within the walls of New Tavern Fort. Whoever the men in the chalk pit were, they had taken some casualties. They might be after revenge. Asif knew the backdoor way into the fort, so we were able to get in and bed down without fuss.

For the first time I felt relaxed enough to think back on our day. Oddly, although we had not seen Pierre, I felt some satisfaction that we had managed to injure at least one of the kidnappers and escape unhurt. So, there was some sense of relief but also the painful realisation that we had failed to find Pierre and at some stage I would have to break this news to Marie.

TWENTY-EIGHT

Deadman's Creek

I AWOKE NEXT MORNING; MY first thought was to tell Gordon about last night's efforts, but he had been sent away to advise on another coastal fortification. I was soon glad that I had stayed within the walls of the fort. Gravesend was abuzz with gossip about gunshots heard at the Swanscombe quarries. It was no surprise to find out that those quarries were owned by the Tibbalds brothers, and that they were now searching for the culprits.

That same morning, I saw the *Spirit of Rochester* sailing down the river towards the estuary. The Excise office confirmed they were bound for Liverpool with a cargo of flint. This must have been a great disappointment to Lynch, who would have been expecting some gold bars hidden amongst it.

Without Gordon, I had no idea what my next move was. I had not heard from Marie, so I assumed she was probably still in Chislehurst. I thought about her a lot. Her absence left a gaping hole in my life.

So, I just pottered about the fort, knowing that my mission might well be coming to an end. There was no more money to support my detective work, no Marie, and still no sign of Pierre. I had reached my nadir. Waves of sadness and disappointment filled my thoughts. Worse, my time with Marie now felt like history, or a dream that had happened to someone else.

A week passed like this. On the seventh day I was sitting by the drill yard inside the fort drinking tea. It was a hot, sunny day but I could not enjoy it. I felt utterly useless and sorry for myself.

Luckily at that moment the fort gate opened. It was Gordon, back from wherever he had been, departing from a hansom cab and as usual making haste to his office. I strode over to greet him.

'Gordon, so good to see you back. Good trip?'

He looked at me without a flicker of emotion. 'Yes, thank you. I will see you in my office in ten minutes.' At that he left me standing on the hot cobbles. Not one for idle gossip was Gordon. It was now the eighth day after the chalk pit fiasco, and I expected Gordon would chastise me for wasting that time. I arrived at his office exactly ten minutes later.

Entering that sparse, cool room, I could see Gordon standing over his desk. As per usual, he got straight to the point.

'Come in Reeves, take a seat, I have some news for you.'

'I must apologise Gordon for what had happened last week at the Swanscombe pits, I thought we had a real chance of making an exchange and getting Pierre back into safe hands.'

Gordon was clearly not that concerned. 'That is all history now. I do not intend to question you on it further. I assume you acted in good faith and any injuries to the Tibbalds gang were self-defence on your part. Am I right?'

I was relieved. 'Yes, sir. Thank you for your understanding.'

'I have received some interesting, but perhaps also worrying, news this morning from the Gravesend police. They have been informed a body of a boy has been washed up at Deadman's Creek, on the way to Cliffe, three miles from here. There is a small chance it could be Pierre, so I thought you might like to take a look with me?'

I answered in the affirmative. This is what I had been dreading. Perhaps the kidnappers in their anger had just killed him and dumped the body in the river. Gordon, pragmatic as ever, had already put things in motion.

'Very well Reeves, I have my horse and trap waiting by the main gate. Let us get going before the body is moved.' At that we departed his office and left the fort.

We headed east from Gravesend along the Rochester road, past the village of Chalk; we were out in the sticks, just farmland with the occasional cottage tucked in by the side of the road. At a junction, we pulled off in the direction of Lower Higham. The countryside here was flat and you could see right over the marshlands to the Thames beyond. We passed Queens Farm, and then took a left in the direction of Shornmead Fort, then crossed over the railway and canal. At that point we reached open windswept marshland and left the main track and headed east across the Shorne marshes. The road to Deadman's Creek was poor, in fact it was scarcely a road at all. Gordon had taken the reins himself but the constant jolting as we made our way down the rutted track made it an unpleasant experience. The creek was out on the marshes, where the land met the river. It was a warm day and above us the seagulls flew towards the estuary. There was no cultivation on this stretch of marshes, just pasture for wandering sheep and cows. The ground itself was very uneven and had probably been salting's till a few years back. The horse had to skirt around the fleets and stagnant ponds, which were overgrown with sedge and bulrush, and of dubious depths. The track meandered over the sections of raised ground where you could safely take a horse and carriage. The higher ground was little more than raised earth mounding alongside water-filled ditches, which perhaps were ancient river defences, long forgotten. A single mistake in your steering and you would be wheel deep in one of those ditches and facing a long delay in retrieving the carriage. Even travelling short distances took time and patience. To our left we could see the Thames and the myriad of shipping which used it every day. As always, it was the barges, with their blood-red sails billowing in the light winds, which stole the show.

Finally, we could see Deadman's Creek in front of us. There was already a pair of policemen there; standing solemnly over something draped in canvas sheeting. The creek was notorious for catching dead bodies. These could be the result of accidents, suicides, or murders. Almost everyone who fell into the river upstream ended up here for some reason. It was an inauspicious place, just mud running out into the river, and a mean shingle beach. There were also the remains of a jetty with its rotting timber posts covered in green moss and seaweed, sticking up vertically out of the mud. Perhaps the jetty was once used as an embarkation point for convicts arriving at the old prison hulks that were moored all around here? What must have those places been like for the convicts during the cold winters? I shivered at the thought.

There was not a single dwelling anywhere near here, just marshland with few trees, and these survivors were bent and strained into contorted shapes by the constant winter winds off the estuary. Despite the heat of the day, this place had a dark, foreboding, feel about it.

Gordon pulled the horse to a stop about a chain away from where the police were standing. He then stepped out onto the shingle beach with me close behind, our boots on the pebbles making a crunching sound as we walked over to the police officers. The policemen seemed unperturbed by our arrival, clearly Gordon was well respected and known by the Gravesend constabulary.

'Hello sir, we were just about to move the body. Can I ask what your interest is in this matter?'

Gordon stood upright. 'Thank you constable for your work in finding the body. This is my associate, William Reeves. He is looking into the disappearance of a thirteen-year-old boy and was concerned that the said body might be that very person. May we have a look at the deceased?'

The constable looked slightly awkward at this request but given Gordon's stature in the town, agreed to it.

'Very well, sir.' He turned to his colleague. 'Bates, lift up the canvas.' The covering was removed and exposed a body, lying in a foetal position, covered in mud. It was a naked boy, who already had signs of rigor mortis that had left his face strangely contorted. There were signs of heavy bruising to his face – these might have been caused by an attack or just the body bumping into objects on its way down the Thames. The mud and detritus picked up from the river also obscured much of his face and body. The policeman clearly felt the need to say something.

'Poor lad. Been dead a good few hours by the look of it, could have come from anywhere. You know what the tides are like round here.'

I stepped closer.

'Can I have a closer look at him?' The policeman nodded. I gently wiped some mud off his face and carefully inspected his facial features. Although approximately the same age and build as Pierre, it was almost impossible to decide if it was the French boy. My only image of him was the photograph that Marie had provided. My gut feeling was that it probably was not him, but I could not be sure. I walked away, then gestured to Gordon that I wanted to be out of the policeman's earshot.

I called over to the officers. 'Can you excuse me – I just need to discuss this with Lieutenant-Colonel Gordon.' The policemen nodded. We walked back to the horse and trap and stood alongside it.

'What do you think Reeves?'

I shrugged. 'I do not think it is Pierre, but I only have one photograph to base this judgement upon. Perhaps once the boy is cleaned up and awaiting the coroner, we could contact Marie-Anne to see if she is willing to visit the mortuary to formally identify the boy?'

Gordon thought for a while. 'Such an action will bring great unhappiness and trepidation to the lady. Are you sure you want to put her through that?'

I replied without hesitation. 'Yes, I think that is necessary.'

Gordon sighed again. 'So be it.' We returned to the policemen and he spoke to them. 'Mr Reeves believes there is a chance that the boy is the son of his client, so we will be requesting that the mother views the body. Where will you be taking him?'

'The deceased will be taken to the temporary mortuary by the assizes on the high street in Gravesend.' Gordon conveyed our thanks for the police's cooperation, and we climbed back onto the trap. We cautiously made our way back towards the fort, the horse and trap wriggling over the winding bunds above the marsh.

He was silent for a while, but then Gordon turned to me. 'You don't really think that boy is Pierre, do you?'

I replied honestly. 'No, on balance I don't think the corpse is Pierre, but I cannot be sure. Perhaps only his mother can confirm his identity – one way or another.'

'I hope Reeves that this is not just a ruse for you to get Marie back in Gravesend? I fear this woman has a hold on you. A dangerous hold, and it is a very worrying game that you are playing.' At that, no more words were spoken. We returned to the fort in silence.

TWENTY-NINE

The Mortuary

LATER THAT MORNING I VISITED Gravesend police station and requested that they telegram Marie; this was on the basis that I believed that the dead boy could be her missing son, Pierre. The police agreed to my request and by the evening I had received a telegram in response stating that Marie would be arriving the next morning at 9 a.m. to identify the body.

The night would give time for the mortuary technician to make the body look half respectable so as not to upset the mother. I had a plan on what I wanted to do when Marie arrived at the mortuary. I spoke to Gordon about this. He was clearly discomforted by my approach but agreed to the course of action. He also knew the officer in charge of the court's cells, which were acting as the temporary mortuary – Jacob Scarfe. He was a good fellow who might be able to help me – if I was discreet.

I did not sleep well that night. I knew I had just one chance to talk with Marie. It would either be when she first arrived at the mortuary, or when she was leaving it after the formal identification. My feelings were that it should be when she left. That would hopefully allow her to see the body and realise it was not Pierre. Obviously if it were Pierre, she would be too distraught to engage in a meaningful conversation. I had no great plan of action but hoped that at this point myself and Asif could find a way of secreting her out of the building.

Asif and I arrived in the high street early, just after eight o'clock, and took our places in the alleyway opposite the court building. Even at this time in the morning the street was busy with people going to and from the market, which was located at the rear of the courts. We waited patiently and just before nine I caught sight of a particularly fine carriage; all my instincts told me that this had come from the French court at Chislehurst. It had come up from West Street, where it turned right onto the high street. It slowly moved uphill towards us. I knew straight away that the carriage belonged to Napoleon because of its stylish livery. I could see Toulouse himself, dressed up to the nines, alongside the driver on top. I assumed Marie was inside the carriage. They must have left Chislehurst at the crack of dawn to get here this early. Clearly Toulouse had decided not to use the train. Whether this was for security reasons, or because arriving in their grandiose carriage was a sign of social status, I do not know. But knowing his character I suspected the latter.

Toulouse stepped down from the driver's seat and went to open the carriage door. As you would expect, he did this with a theatrical flourish. Clearly he thought his presence in Gravesend was an important event for the town.

Little did he know that his day was going to be ruined! At this moment, while Toulouse was blindsided by the coach, I slipped out of the alley and crossed the road in front of the carriage heading for the market. The Frenchman was too engaged in opening the door to notice me. I grabbed a quick glance back. Yes, there she was – Marie, dressed in black, stepping down gracefully from the carriage, with Toulouse holding her hand to make safe her step.

I carried on towards the market, but then instead of walking in, entered the side door of the court building. This had been left unlocked for my convenience. In the foyer of the building stood Jacob Scarfe. From his features and demeanour, I could see he was a very decent man. He gestured for me to take the stairs down to the cells, which I did without delay. I was just in time, as I could hear the front door opening and the arrival of Marie and Toulouse. At the bottom of the stairs I came upon a short corridor. The basement was a spartan affair; on the left were three cells, and the door of the middle one was open. Glancing in, I could see a body, lying on a slab in the centre of the room. The cellblock was cold, almost perfect conditions for a dead body but horrible for the living. Luckily, there were no other people there. I noted the lavatory at the far end of the corridor, and swiftly secreted myself inside it. After a few seconds' wait, I could hear voices, albeit indistinctly and the sound of the footsteps. I guessed that Scarfe, Marie and Toulouse were coming down the stairs.

I could just make out some indistinct chatter, so I assumed that the three of them were walking along the corridor. After a pause, Marie was led into the cell containing the body. Luckily, they left the cell door open so I could hear what was being said. There was a long pause. Then I clearly heard Marie's voice. 'It is not Pierre. Praise be to God.'

Simple as that. Toulouse then spoke in his usual pretentious, authoritative voice. 'Very well, thank you for your time Mr Scarfe, but it appears we have been on a wasted trip.'

Scarfe replied. 'No problem at all sir if I can be of anymore—'

He stopped mid-sentence. Suddenly his hushed, kindly tones were drowned out by noise from outside. It sounded as if there was a kafuffle in the street.

Toulouse urgently broke into the conversation. 'I think our carriage is being attacked, can you excuse me, while I sort this out?'

I could hear his heavy footsteps running up the stairs. I knew what was occurring. As per the plan Asif had jumped onto the coach, pushed off the driver and was attempting to steal the carriage. The ensuing noise and hullaballoo had reached Toulouse's ears. I took my chance. I threw open the door of the privy and stood in front of Scarfe and Marie. She looked shocked beyond measure.

Scarfe knew of my intentions so took it in his stride. Marie spoke first. 'What are you doing here, what is going on?'

Scarfe said knowingly, 'I will leave you to it then, you know the back way out Mr Reeves.'

I smiled. 'Yes, thanks.' Scarfe walked up the stairs leaving us alone. I looked at Marie, I was now so close. 'Marie, please we have no time. Follow me, out of here, and I'll tell you what you need to know.'

Marie's response was not what I expected, not at all. 'I'm not going anywhere until you tell me what is going on.'

I felt desperation. 'Please Marie, Toulouse will be back soon, we only have seconds.'

She stood her ground. 'Have you done this? Brought me here to Gravesend on a wild goose chase? You knew that boy was not my Pierre, you have seen his photograph, yet you still did this. How could you? I have lain awake all night, my stomach twisted in pain, thinking my boy was dead. How could you be so cruel?'

I was now at my wits' end, I continued unabashed. 'But how else could I get you out of Chislehurst? How could I get you back with me? Look we can run, we can get out the back of this building, find somewhere to hide, then when the coast is clear, start a new life.'

Her face said it all, I did not need her words – but they came anyway. 'You are a fool William, my allegiance is with the Emperor, he is my rock, not you. When he has recovered from his operation he will see how important I am to him, and I will take my place as the true Empress. I cannot risk all that and live like a fugitive, with a man who has no prospects.'

I stood dumbfounded. A sword through my heart would have hurt less. 'I'm sorry Marie, I thought we had something special. Please forgive me for this subterfuge. I just hoped that we could be together.'

She softened a moment. 'I do understand William, and I'm very fond of you but I must think of my future.'

I was not giving up. 'We can have a future. The Emperor will die soon, everyone knows that.' Marie winced. 'He is not your future. Look, can we make a deal? If I can find your son and bring him to you, would that be proof enough of my love?'

She seemed perplexed by my offer but finally agreed. 'Very well William. If you can do that, then I will know you are a real man. A man as big as the Emperor. If you can get my Pierre back, I will give you my heart. But not before.' At this point I could hear noise from the foyer above and footsteps on the stairs. I reached over and gently kissed her outstretched hand, then darted back into the lavatory. I could hear from within the cubicle Toulouse talking to Marie.

'I am very a sorry for that my lady, we had some lascar idiot trying to steal the carriage. He has run off now. So, all is well. Are you ready to depart?' She answered in the affirmative, and I could hear their footsteps going up the stairs. I was left alone with my thoughts. I waited a few minutes then slipped out. The carriage had now gone. I thanked Scarfe profusely for his help and walked out onto the high street.

I soon came upon a bloodied Asif. 'Mr Reeves, why are you here? Why did she not want to go away with you?'

I sighed. 'I really don't know Asif; women can be strange creatures. Thanks for your help though, at least I got to speak to her. Now let us get back to the fort and get you cleaned up.'

THIRTY

The Next Move

I WAS NOW BACK AT the fort but utterly bereft. All my dreams were turning to ashes. I now had a stark choice – give up on Pierre and Marie, and go back to my old life, or carry on trying to achieve what felt like the impossible.

I spoke to Gordon about my quandary. He was transparent in his attitude, he felt that I should now cut my losses and forget about Marie and the lost boy. I racked my conscience – was my love for Marie causing me to lose my judgement? Finally, I concluded that on this occasion I would let my heart rule my head and try one more roll of the dice. I would take Asif to meet Jack Carter and confront him with the truth about his son. Maybe, just maybe, Jack might have some key information that he had withheld up to now.

So, that afternoon we walked up to his modest house near the top of Windmill Hill. For once Asif was a little nervous. I knocked on the door and waited. Finally, the grizzly old seaman appeared, there was no great smile of recognition or welcome on his face. He seemed to be wearing the same jumper as the last time I had seen him, despite the warm July weather.

'What do you want?' he snapped.

I smiled back. 'Let me introduce my friend, Asif, who has been assisting me since I came to Gravesend.'

Asif reached out to shake Jack's hand; the offer of the handshake was brushed aside. 'I'm not shaking a lascar's hand. What's your business?'

'Jack, we would just like to talk to you some more. We also could have some information that might be of interest to you.'

'I've told you everything I know about that night when the French lad was supposed to have come ashore. Now leave me alone.'

I maintained an even tone of voice and continued, 'It is not information from you we want. It is information we have, that might be of interest to you.' I lowered the tone of my voice. 'About the death of your boy, Tom.'

Jack's expression dropped, like he had been slapped in the face. 'How would you know anything about all that? Be off with you.'

'Asif was on the same boat as your boy, ten years ago, on the spice run from India. He remembers his illness and death. I thought that might be of interest to you. Now, can we come in?'

Jack had now lost his granite-hard exterior – his dead son was clearly his Achilles heel. He looked visibly upset.

'You had better come in then.'

We were ushered inside and sat down in his parlour as directed. Jack clearly had no time for pleasantries today, he was obviously upset that his son's death had been mentioned at all.

'Go on then, tell me what you know. And if this is a trick, there will be trouble.'

I looked at Asif, then back to Jack. 'It is my friend here, Asif, who has the information which you may find of interest. Go ahead Asif.'

Though nervous, he cleared his throat and spoke well. 'I was waiting for a boat to work on in Zanzibar. This was ten years ago. Captain Lynch arrived in port with the *Spirit of Rochester*, a fine ship. The captain grabbed any men interested in becoming crew and put us on board. He did not care if we knew what we were doing or got hurt. We work very hard. It was rush, rush, rush – get to London quickly. The sooner there, the bigger the profit. So, Captain Lynch was cutting all corners to get to England fast. It was my first voyage, so I remember everything that happened. The smell of the boat. The names of the crewmen and officers.' He paused for a moment to get his breath. 'I remember Mr Carter; he was a junior officer and was already in the sick bay when we sailed out of Zanzibar.' Jack was having none of this.

'Nonsense, it's a fact that Tom was not ill till they put into Freetown, in Sierra Leone. That was in the coroner's report, and the captain's log.'

I could see this was going to hurt the old sea lag, but he needed to know. I took up the story.

'I'm afraid Asif is telling the truth, as he saw it. I have been working with him for the last few weeks and know him to be an honest man worthy of total trust. Now Asif, continue with your story.'

'Mr Carter was sick all the way around the African coast. I think it was malaria he had, though I did not know for sure as we were kept apart from the officers – who seemed upset at what was going on. I was told they pleaded with Captain Lynch to drop anchor in Cape Town to allow him to go into a hospital, but he insisted there was no time to lose and raced on. By the time we berthed at Freetown, it was too late, Mr Carter had died from malaria.'

Jack's face dropped and there was a look of deep sadness, as if he were close to tears.

'I'd like to be left alone,' he said.

I nodded. 'Of course, I understand. We will let ourselves out.'

We got up and respectfully made our way slowly back to the front door. Just as we got there, Carter turned back to us.

'So that is what really happened? You're telling me that if Lynch had not been so greedy, Tom could have been saved?'

Asif replied, 'Yes, sir, that is my opinion.'

There were a few moments' pause. Finally, Jack said; 'Sit down you two. What can I do for you? If it gets Lynch locked up, I'll help you in any way I can.'

We returned to the parlour and sat down again. I opened the conversation.

'I am sorry to bring you that news, but we desperately need your help. We must find the French boy, and you are our last hope. Have you any idea, any thoughts as to what may have occurred? Is there any place he could be hidden in the town?'

Carter took out his pipe and lit it slowly with a long match. He inhaled deeply – though the tobacco had hardly taken. There was a long pause, I noticed the smell of the house, a mixture of mustiness and stale tobacco – finally he spoke. 'I've been thinking about that as well, since I saw you. Something was playing on the back of my mind. Then I remembered. It is a long shot but maybe worth looking into. Tunnels. There are smugglers' tunnels running from near the pier up into the town. They were used by smugglers right up to the 1830s. I went down them when I was a boy. They got blocked off when the smuggling ended, but they still might exist. That would be a good place to hide someone. Not very pleasant though.'

I almost gasped in excitement; this could be the breakthrough we needed. 'Have you any more information on the exact location of these tunnels?'

Carter held up his finger. 'Give me a minute, I think I've got a map somewhere.' He stood up and walked over to his bureau. Although of modest dimensions, Jack's house had good-quality furniture, with dark brown mahogany timber everywhere. Similar to the inside of a captain's cabin. In fact, his furnishings might have well come from such a source. After much shuffling and searching, a double foolscap map appeared. He brought it out and spread it on the table.

'Here we are, a street map of the riverside area, and as you can see I've drawn in pencil the approximate location of the tunnels.'

I studied the map in as much detail as I could understand. Jack could see my excitement so added some words of caution. 'The map is old now, so some of these tunnels may have been filled in, others adapted to become sewers or what have you.'

I looked hard at the map; the details of the streets overlaid by the pencil markings of the tunnels. My eyes were drawn to the riverside area. 'Look here.' I pointed to the junction of the high street with Gravesend pier. It looked like there might be a tunnel running under the King's Arms.

'Is it possible that a tunnel might be connected to the beer cellar of the King's Arms?'

Jack puffed his pipe and stroked his chin thoughtfully.

'It is possible, but you cannot be sure, the map is over forty years old, anything could have happened since.'

I nodded. 'I think I've seen enough to give it a try. I'll need to get into the cellar and have a poke about of course, but it's definitely worth a go.' I held out my hand. 'Thank you very much Mr Carter, and I'm sorry I had to bring you such news of your son.'

'To be honest, I'm not surprised. Typical of Lynch to put the chance of profit before a man's life. Promise me this though; if you get this French lad back, make sure you get Lynch sent down for his part in it. Can you do that?'

'Yes, I'll make sure of that. Thank you for your help.'

At that he did something I was not expecting, he held out his hand, inviting a handshake from Asif. My friend was obviously delighted. They shook hands. 'Thank you for your candour Asif. I'm glad you knew of my boy.'

At that he returned to the parlour, leaving us to go out of the front door. Outside of the darkness of the house, the sunlight seemed even brighter than usual. I closed the door behind us and turned to Asif.

'I think we are finally in with a chance now. Come on, let us get things organised.'

At that we walked down Windmill Hill back towards the fort. It was still a fine warm afternoon as we strode down the hill. We did not talk but I had now begun to realise how much I owed Asif; without his devotion and skill, I would be lost.

'What are you going to do when your work at the fort ends?'

He seemed unperturbed by this. 'I will find another ship, go back to sea. Find my way back home. Something will turn up.'

I smiled. 'Indeed, who knows what tomorrow holds.'

At the bottom of the hill we passed the Customs office and at that point I heard the heavy hoofs of a pair of dray horses, behind us. I was glad to see it was Jessie Armitage on his delivery run. I shouted over to him. 'Jessie, any chance of a quick word?' He gently tugged at the reins and brought the pair to a stop, then jumped down.

'What can I do for you Mr Reeves?'

I gestured for us to get out of earshot of his second man, so we walked away from his dray, and stopped under the shade of a London Plane tree.

'Jessie, I wonder if you could do me a big favour?'

He listened attentively. 'What would that be Mr Reeves?'

I said, 'I need the key to the street cellar door for the King's Arms. Can you get hold of it for me?'

Jessie looked a little concerned but obviously still wanted to help. 'What would you be wanting that for?'

I gently pulled him closer to me so that I was almost speaking into his ear. 'We believe that the French boy may be incarcerated in tunnels below the pub, which can only be reached from the beer cellar. If we can get in there tonight, we could have a rummage around and try and find that tunnel.'

Jessie looked genuinely concerned at this. 'Begging your pardon sir but I've only just been allowed back onto the drays after the break-in at the brewery. I would not want to do anything that might come back on me.'

I was not happy at this but had to agree. 'Very well Jessie. I understand how important your job is to you, but I am disappointed at your response.'

'Thing is sir, I don't know why Mr Gordon insisted I should turn a blind eye to your robbery in the first place. I am none the wiser. All I know is that you went into John Bennett's office. I saw that out of the corner of my eye.'

I decided to tell all. 'The truth is, Jessie, that we were just looking through Bennett's files to make a link between Tommy Tibbalds' keg business and the King's Arms, we found that. We also found something more disturbing. I do not want to upset you, but I think you need to know what kind of man Bennett is. To put it bluntly, we found a file containing numerous photographs of young boys in stages of undress and in some cases… performing sexual acts.'

I stood stock still waiting for Jessie's reaction. He was clearly mortified. 'That dirty bastard! I'll kill him!'

'Let us leave that to the police. Taking out a personal vengeance will do no one any good.'

Jessie was still shaking with rage, so I continued. 'We are fairly sure that Bennett and Lynch had some kind of sex ring involving boys. Once we have the full proof of that, they will reap the whirlwind, you have my word for that.'

Jessie was still red-faced and upset. He tried to speak but stumbled over his words. 'You don't think they used my boy like that do you?' He looked imploring at me for an answer.

'I'm sorry Jessie I just don't know'.

We both stood in silence for a moment, then he turned to me. 'About the key. That will be no problem. I will slip it in my pocket and bring it to you after my shift. Anything that helps put those bastards away.'

I looked at him with concern, I knew my words had crushed his world, but felt I had no choice. 'Thank you Jessie.'

He seemed to calm down a little and spoke more purposefully. 'I'll do all I can to help you and get you that for key tonight. Shall I meet you by the river, in front of the Clarendon? I walk home that way after work. Say, five o'clock?'

I smiled. 'That would be great Jessie, and if we succeed we will owe you a great deal.' He was now getting over the shock.

'If you get that boy back with his parents, it will help make up for me losing my George, and it will be one in the eye for Lynch and his scummy friends. I'll see you later.'

At that he swiftly made his way back onto the high seat of the dray, said a few words to his second man, and grabbing the reins gingered the horses into life. Within seconds the heavy horses were trotting off down the street. One wave of his bowler hat and he was gone.

I turned to Asif. 'It looks as if it is a runner tonight. Let us get back to the fort and prepare.'

THIRTY-ONE
Riverside Sightings

ASIF AND I MADE OUR way down to the Clarendon's riverfront just before 5 p.m. It had been a warm day, the river was like a millpond, seemingly unaffected by tides. Despite the lack of a breeze, more craft were coming upriver, mostly Thames barges, catching the meagre winds with their fully erect blood-red sails. I took in all these sights and smells. The Thames was probably the busiest commercial waterway in the world, but on a late afternoon like this, it seemed serene and untroubled.

I turned to Asif; he was the most engaging of companions. Nothing ever seemed to trouble or defeat him. He seemed to have an understanding of his own destiny which I envied. I spoke. ' Don't you ever get homesick? This is a very foreign country to you after all.'

'No sir, I can look at the sea before me and know it is the same sea that will take me back to my homeland one day. It will all come to pass when the time is right.'

And that was that. We just stood there, taking in the warmth of the sun. Then I noticed Asif stir, like a hawk seeing its prey.

'Look, sir.' He pointed downriver at the bend of the Thames known as the Hope. My eyes were immediately drawn to what he had seen. A big sailing ship, coming up the estuary, just rounding Hope Point towed by a steam tug. It was an old square-rigged sailing ship, a china clipper, there was only one boat it could be. The *Spirit of Rochester*.

'What is it doing back here Asif? I thought we'd seen the last of her for a long while.'

He shook his head. 'I do not know.'

I thought back to the fiasco at the chalk pits; that had been ten days ago. 'It must have got to Liverpool in good time, unloaded its flint for the potteries, and come straight back here.'

Asif looked bemused 'Why would it be doing that?'

I shrugged. 'I don't know, maybe they are bringing a load down south to London. Perhaps earthenware from the potteries. Who knows?'

Asif look concerned.

'Will it spoil our plans if he stops here?'

'It will make no difference. If we strike at the cellar in the middle of the night, Lynch and his crew will be fast asleep.' At that we relaxed and awaited the arrival of Jessie.

On the stroke of five he arrived. He was out of his dark green uniform livery. Now, he was just another man on the street. 'Good evening Mr Reeves, I've got the key here.'

At that he surreptitiously took the key from his pocket and passed it to me. 'Be careful with that and let me have it back before trouble breaks. Remember, I am doing this for the boy. Don't take anything else from the cellar.'

I nodded in agreement. 'Of course not. You have my word on that.' At this point Jessie noticed Asif staring at the sailing ship creeping upriver and asked, 'Is that the boat that was here before, Lynch's ship, the *Spirit of Rochester*?'

'Indeed,' I said.

Jessie's face darkened. 'I might have a word with that Mr Lynch when I see him.'

I hastened caution. 'Please do not confront him until this night is over, I would not want him forewarned in any way. Look, you have done your bit to help. Getting Pierre out and pinning his abduction on Lynch is the best way to get even with him.'

'Very well Mr Reeves, but if I did want a word, any idea where his haunts are in the town?' I was still a little concerned at telling him too much but needed to keep him on our side.

'In all likelihood he will be drinking himself stupid at the King's Arms tonight with his cronies. Probably first thing in the morning, when the Customs office opens, he will turn up with his paperwork, like the well-respected sea captain he is.'

Asif smiled at my sarcasm.

Jessie seemed content now. 'Very well Mr Reeves, Asif.'

He shook our hands. 'I'll be on my way.'

At that he departed and made his way home. I looked at Asif and the *Spirit*, coming ever closer to the town on the tide. 'I think I have seen enough of that boat to last me a lifetime. Let us make sure we do our job right at the cellar and find the evidence to put Lynch away for good.' At that we strode off back to the fort, to make our preparations for the night.

THIRTY-TWO

Dark Places
for Dark Deeds

IT WAS THREE HOURS PAST midnight when Asif and I took the short walk from the fort to the King's Arms. I had organised some tools to help us – a Davey lamp, jemmy, rope ladder and some other odds and ends. With that equipment, we did not want to be stopped by any overenthusiastic peeler. Luckily the streets were empty. Nobody. No constabulary, or lost sailors; not even the whores who came down with each new ship arrival. It was a still night, so sound would carry easily so we had to be careful. Reaching the King's Arms, we paused by the cellar hatches. These were the usual route for beer deliveries, and luckily we had the key. There was just enough moonlight to see the dusty keyhole. Gently unlocking the rusting iron lock, we prised the timber flaps open and stared inside. We stopped to listen.

Still no sound.

We had brought a rope ladder, and with Asif taking the weight, I climbed down into the cellar. I made a slight thumping noise as I hit the stone floor but nothing to worry about. The cellar was dark, but I could just make out, all around me, the paraphernalia of a public house. Beer barrels were everywhere, and crates of bottled beer were stacked against the damp brick walls. The cellar was perhaps seven feet to ceiling height so I guessed we could escape by just standing on a barrel, so I bade Asif to come down and dispense with the rope ladder. He manoeuvred himself through the hatch, closing it behind him as he did so, with me underneath him, taking the weight of his body to give a soft landing.

We were now both standing in the cellar; what next? I had brought a small Davey lamp with me, which I lit. It sizzled slightly but I was pleased to see there was enough air in the cellar to make a good light. We could now see more clearly the outlines of the space around us. I had taken in all the information from Carter's map, which seemed to indicate that the tunnel, if it still existed, would be located somewhere to the east side of the cellar. I gingerly walked over to that area, making sure not to trip on any hidden hazards, and inspected the exposed wall. There were no obvious signs of an opening, no new areas of brickwork which might indicate the bricking up of a tunnel. However, much of the wall was hidden behind a stack of beer crates. I prodded at the crates. They were quart bottles, four to a case. Nothing odd there. Then Asif spotted something. He tapped me on the shoulder and pointed out that two of the crates, at the bottom of the stack were full of empty bottles, and dusty bottles at that. Why had these been left so long?

Bottles had a value. I then noticed that the crates directly above the bottom two were also full of empty bottles. I gently tugged at a crate. I fully expected it to be stuck firm, weighed down by those above but instead it just slid out. In fact, all four crates, on the first and second tiers, slid out without fuss. I could see the crates above the second tier were in fact held up by a hidden shelf, which took their weight. With the crates removed I could see a square of timber embedded within the brickwork, just two feet or so square. This must be a hidden doorway, small in width but big enough for a man to crawl through. The door had some kind of lock. I had no key for it, so set about it with the jemmy. It was an awkward task, trying to wrench this door open while not making noise but eventually it gave, and I was able to open the timber door.

We could now see in front of us a tunnel, slightly wider than the entrance door but still tight. The tunnel, though narrow, was perfectly constructed with brickwork walls and timber boarded roof. It had clearly been there for many years as I noted the bricks were handmade and irregular, not the modern machine-made kind. I hate confined spaces but had to get into it. I crawled in first, followed by Asif. Thank God for the lamp. In the near darkness my other senses became sharper and I began to smell things. I detected the odour of stale food or was it sewage? We crawled along the tunnel noting how unpleasant this space was. After about twenty feet the tunnel went around a ninety-degree bend and then opened out into an underground room, about ten feet square, with perhaps six feet head height. I gratefully got out of the tunnel and stood up. My legs were much relieved to be doing their proper job. I assumed we would now be under West Street itself, but it did not matter. Here in the underground we were in a totally separate world, unconnected to the normality above. We stood there, staring around in the dark, musty, cavern of a room.

That is when I detected a smell.

There was another human being in this space.

It could only be the boy.

I was aware of a presence, so waved the lamp in front of my face to try to adjust my eyes to the dim light. Then I saw him. Lying on a straw bed in the corner, with nothing but a piss pot and a small, unlit candle beside him. I let out the word 'Pierre'. The boy slowly came to life. His face was gaunt. He was thin and dressed in rags. His face looked ashen. A look of terror crossed his face. I spoke as gently as I could. 'Pierre we are here for you. Your mother, Marie, sent us, we are here for you.' The boy looked back in a state of shock and disbelief. His pale face was gaunt, and his eyes were dead – he had already suffered too much. I tried again saying *'Bonjour'*.

In the weakest of voices, he replied, *'Bonjour'*. He was in a state. I walked over to where he lay, and gently helped him to his feet. He was painfully thin, his legs looked as though rickets had set in. Just getting him to his feet was not easy. He smelt of months of not washing. Asif joined me and together we took him under his arms, and started to half walk, half drag him out of that place. I could see the state he was in. His clothes were rotten, and he smelt badly. Hardly surprising but I had to fight back the nausea and concentrate on getting him out of this hellhole.

Asif was a godsend, so strong and completely nonplussed by the situation. We got him into the narrower tunnel, Asif went first with the lamp dragging Pierre behind him with me at the rear, gently pushing him on. It was hard graft pushing and pulling the deadweight of Pierre but eventually we got through. Within a few minutes we were out of the narrow tunnel and into the cellar and able to stand upright again. We got Pierre to his feet, but he could scarcely hold the strength to stand up. Nevertheless, we carried on and got him to the closed cellar trapdoors. Now we would have to somehow manhandle him up into the street. At that moment, there was a tap on the cellar hatch above. I froze momentarily but then with much relief, heard our friend Jessie's voice.

'Are you alright down there?'

'Yes, we've got the lad but he's weak, open the hatch, and help us lift him out.'

Within seconds the hatches were opened, and I could see, by the light of my lamp, Jessie's smiling face in the darkness. I could also smell the fresh air from the world outside the cellar.

'I couldn't sleep, so I came to see if I could help,' he said.

'Thanks,' I replied, grateful for his presence.

We took the weight of Pierre's body and lifted him up to a height where Jessie could pull him out. Then standing on a nearby keg, we climbed out.

It was a relief to get out of that hellhole. Jessie closed the hatch. We looked around; the street was still quiet. In a couple of hours, it would be dawn and the knocker uppers would be out, but for now we had the town to ourselves.

'Let us get him back to the fort,' I said.

Myself and Asif then tried walking him, with our shoulders under his arms to take the weight, but he was clearly not comfortable with that and his feet dragged on the floor. Asif stopped. 'I can take him myself sir, he is only light.' At that he put his arm between Pierre's legs and lifted him over his shoulder. 'I will carry him to the fort.'

At that he strode off, clearly unhindered by the boy's weight. I stood by the cellar door with Jessie and turned to him. 'Thanks for your help, you don't need to be involved anymore, we can take it from here.'

Jessie looked at me, his face seemed contorted in pain now. 'That poor lad, it looks as if he has been stuck in that tunnel for months. How can they have been so cruel?'

'I know Jessie, it is inhuman, disgusting. Let us hope that they didn't abuse him as well. This is the dark side of humanity, no doubt about that.' I added more cheerfully, 'But you have helped us save him, hopefully.'

Asif was now out of sight making good progress along West Street in the direction of the fort. Jessie clearly had more to say, though I could not tarry long.

'Do you think that is what those bastards did to my boy, used him like a toy, an animal?'

I replied honestly. 'I really don't know.' Jessie was clearly distraught but gestured towards Asif disappearing with Pierre down the road. 'You had better make sure he's safe.' With that he disappeared into the night.

I could not hang around. I would have liked more time to pacify Jessie and make things better for him, but I had to make sure we got the boy back to the fort safely, so I scampered off in that direction. I need not have worried. Asif seemed to be carrying Pierre effortlessly. So much so that I was out of breath by the time I caught up with them. By now we had reached the fort's outer door. I opened it with my key and we soon had the boy lying down in the sick bay area. There were no medical orderlies around at this time, so Asif and I sat quietly by the boy. He seemed unable to talk, even react to us normally, but we offered him some water, which he took.

We sat with him for an hour or so until dawn broke. Gordon was up and about early and immediately came over to the sick bay to ascertain the position. He entered the room and a look of deep sadness crossed his face as he saw the gaunt, almost lifeless figure of Pierre.

'Well done Reeves, you did it! I can see the boy's in a bad state though. I'll get the fort's medical officer in here straight away.' At that he strode out. We looked down at Pierre; it was not even clear if the lad would live, let alone be in a fit state to hand back to Marie.

The medical orderly was roused from his sleep. He hurriedly set about seeing to the boy. We were asked to leave the room as he did a thorough investigation, or as thorough as you can be when the patient is almost comatose. Ten minutes later we were ushered back in. Gordon had now re-joined us. The orderly was of typical military bearing, his name was Broadhurst, and he had a fine dark moustache which compensated for his receding hairline. He stood six feet tall, and rapier straight.

He spoke. 'I'm afraid the boy is in a bad way. Clear signs of malnutrition, rickets, some fever, also rashes on his backside. His mental health is also suspect. I am not getting very much response. I can only suggest either hospitalisation, or complete rest and a diet of broth, water, and small portions of food. Perhaps some fruit jelly or similar when he's ready.' He finished and stood with his arms clasped behind his waistband. Gordon seemed content with this.

'Very well Broadhurst, thank you for that. I think, gentlemen, we will keep him here for the time being and follow the regime suggested. Are we all in agreement?' I was not entirely happy with that, so stated my case.

'The boy has a mother who is deeply concerned at his whereabouts. Can I contact her and arrange for her to come here?'

Gordon looked slightly awkward, he turned to the medical orderly. 'That will be all Broadhurst.' The officer without delay left the room.

Gordon still seemed deep in thought. 'We have to be careful about how we handle this. The boy being in the fort must be kept secret from the public and particularly the local press. However, I think it would be safe for you to contact the mother to say, in general terms, that her boy is safe, and that a reunion will be forthcoming.'

I smiled. 'Thank you sir.'

Gordon seemed content now. 'But please do not give the location of Pierre to the mother, and could you use the post office telegram office. I do not want any publicity about this.' I smiled. That was enough for now. Gordon made to leave but at the last moment looked back at myself and Asif.

'By the way, I must congratulate you on what you have achieved. I did not think this was possible, I thought the boy was dead, now I see he is alive, and that is because of your perseverance. May God bless you.'

At this he left the room, leaving me and Asif pleasantly surprised by his kind words.

THIRTY-THREE

The Aftermath

WITHIN THE HOUR BROADHURST HAD returned, so relieving myself and Asif. I went back to my room to wash and shave and Asif went off to his work in the grounds – the man was a godsend. I then had some simple breakfast of tea, bread and jam which brought the time around to almost nine o'clock. I was not sure when the post office opened but it should be by now. Government offices, included the Excise House and Royal Mail office, were usually open by nine. So, I set out to walk to the post office, in the town centre. It was a glorious morning; I had not slept but felt elated. I had done it. Now perhaps Marie might look twice at me.

Striding out through the fort door I could see the corner of the Customs and Excise offices, located at the end of a street called The Terrace, which ran parallel to the river. To my left, running at ninety degrees to The Terrace, and climbing up to the town centre, was a tree-lined thoroughfare named Milton Place, which boasted fine, white-rendered Georgian houses along its town side. The morning sun warmed my back. All in all, this was perhaps one of the best mornings of my life. Then, something caught the corner of my eye. Stopped on Milton Place was a brewer's dray, with the horses drinking out off a stone trough by the side of the road. Surprisingly, and coincidentally, I could see the driver was Jessie himself. I waved over to him but decided not to go and talk to him as familiarity might breed gossip about last night's affair.

Oddly, he did not wave back to me. Ignoring this, I strode out along The Terrace, passing the Customs House, which was just opening for business. There was something strange though. I thought back. Why was Jessie on the dray on his own – he usually had a second man? Maybe the man was running an errand or something. I thought no more about it. Then low and behold, who should I see walking up the street towards me, but Captain John Lynch and John Bennett. For a moment I froze, then realised they were not that interested in me. They were bringing paperwork to the Customs office. This was often the first port of call for returning sea captains. I decided to front them out if anything was said, so carried on walking. They had not noticed me yet anyway. Then something unexpected happened. I could hear heavy horses behind me. I turned around. Just in time. It was Jessie, with his fully laden dray coming down Milton Place at a gallop. With infinite skill he swung the dray around the dogleg corner of Milton Place, and came into The Terrace. He was moving at a pace and to my surprise, then accelerated further. I could see Jessie now, standing up, whipping the two dray horses. They were now careering down the road at breakneck speed! The air was filled with the sound of the galloping, sweating horses, and Jessie's whip, urging them on. They shot past my side, narrowly missing me. And the horses were still picking up speed! In front of me, some forty yards distant, were Lynch and Bennett, walking in my direction. Too late they realised what was happening. The dray, now moving at an unstoppable speed, was heading straight towards them!

At the last moment, the horses edged left, but this only made the two men's fate even more certain. The fully loaded dray slid sideways, with the heavy cart, full of beer barrels, crashing into them. They had no chance. Their bodies were crushed between the cart and the brick wall alongside the footpath. There were cries of agony and shock. The driver was thrown clear, an enormous distance –perhaps thirty feet – crashing into the cobblestones. The bewildered horses seemed to have escaped serious injury but were now in a state of total panic.

I ran down to the scene. Both Lynch's and Bennett's bodies were smashed; broken between the cart and the wall. Both must be dead, as their injuries were unspeakable. I looked over to Jessie. He was clearly injured but alive. The whole scene was carnage, frightened horses rearing up, broken beer kegs, smashed wheels, and axles. And, trapped by the brick wall, maimed bodies. In fact, the scene was indescribable.

People came to help. Clerks from the Customs House, passers-by, then eventually solders from the fort. The horses were calmed, sheets were thrown over the dead men. Jessie was taken by ambulance cart to the nearest hospital. I was by now almost wandering around the scene in a state of shock. True, I had often wished Lynch and Bennett dead, but not like this. I could hear people gossiping. Clearly they thought that it had been a case of the horses running out of control, bolting down the terrace. Just a terrible, terrible accident. But I knew only too well what had occurred.

Gordon had appeared from the fort and saw me floundering. 'Reeves, let us get you back inside. You need some sweet tea.' I hesitated, then realising Gordon's words were an order, not a request, I followed him back and he led me to the sanctuary of his office.

I was sat down in his office. I recounted what had occurred and what I believe had been Jessie's motive. Clearly none of this was music to Gordon's ears. 'This is a total disaster; you realise that Reeves.'

I stared back at him, unable to raise the words. 'Did you contact the mother about Pierre?'

'No, I was on my way to the post office when it happened.'

He breathed deeply. 'Good. From now on we will have to make the boy's presence in the fort top secret. Two men at least have died, possibly murder by the sound of it. There will be a coroner's report, perhaps a criminal trial. The evidence, and motive, might come back to you, and by association myself. When you got involved in all of this I explained how delicate international relations were with France, how we could not countenance any obvious involvement in the affairs of the French court in exile. Now we have two possible murders to deal with.'

He stood up and paced around the room. At length he spoke.

'Leave this to me. This is what will happen now. On no account contact Marie. It would also be prudent for you to leave the fort and go back to London. Do I make myself clear?'

I answered in the affirmative.

'Obviously, the constabulary may well wish to interview you, depending on what Jessie Armitage says to them. We shall of course make sure Pierre is well looked after. If anyone asks, we shall say he is an orphan found half drowned in the river. No mention shall be made of the French connection. Is that all clear?'

I stuttered, 'Yes, sir and thank you for—'

He stopped me dead. 'Do not thank me. I have done my Christian duty, that is all – let us hope that there is no price to pay for that. Now go and pack your bags.' I looked at Gordon, then without any handshake walked out of his office.

I was shocked but knew I had to accede to his demands. I left the fort, left Gravesend that day. I said my sad farewells to Asif and some of the other friends I had made there. At midday I was on the ferry back across the river and from Tilbury Fort station, caught the train back to London. My time on the riverside was over but I would keep my promise and not contact Marie… Not yet anyway.

THIRTY-FOUR

New Starts

IT WAS WITH A HEAVY heart that I returned to my shared rooms, near the Bell Foundry in Whitechapel. Luckily, my brother was on permanent night shift at the printers in Fleet Street, so I did not need to make small talk with him. I could just stare out of my bedroom window at the constant activity on the Whitechapel Road, of people coming in and out of London.

Our rooms were in the best part of Whitechapel, and we were surrounded by fairly successful tradesman. However, the dirt-poor parts of the locality were just a stone's throw away. The city was busy, always busy now. There was the constant clatter of horses and carriages passing by my window. There was so much horse manure left in their wake I often wished I had a garden, so that I could collect the dung with a bucket and spade and spread it on the soil. No such luck. I was stuck in first-floor rooms, looking out over the main London-bound road.

I had a mountain of paperwork to catch up on, which included a written statement to the Gravesend Police recounting the events of that fateful morning when Lynch and Bennett perished. It always amazed me, the fragility of life. One moment they had been strutting down the sunlit street, a wealthy sea captain and his agent, the next instant and they were just bloodied meat and bones. Extinguished.

I wondered how Jessie was doing but dare not ask. However, I guessed that at some stage the constabulary would want more from me. The idea that the deaths were just some tragic traffic accident really did not stick. Everyone in the town knew Lynch and Bennett had enemies so there was bound to be a serious police investigation into their deaths.

I also worried about Pierre, how was his recovery going, and how soon could I contact Marie? My love for her was giving me sleepless nights. I had hoped my mind might find interests elsewhere, but if anything, our separation was making things worse, I could not get her out of my head.

Two weeks had passed since my leaving Gravesend. It was a Saturday and, though late July, the rain was pouring relentlessly down the windowpanes. It had rained all night, then all day, so even my restless walks had been put on hold. In Whitechapel many of the shops were now owned by Jewish immigrants, so Saturday, their sabbath, was a noticeably quiet day. I tried to read but nothing could take my mind off Marie. Things were getting worse, not better.

In Chislehurst Marie looked out of her bedroom window. It was Saturday morning, but only 4 a.m., dawn had yet to rise but she felt unable to sleep. It had been raining all night and this had made her room feel damp and cold. She had now been under virtual house arrest for over two weeks.

Toulouse had cut her off from everyone. From the other staff, from looking after the ailing Emperor – everything. She was not even allowed to read newspapers. She was in total limbo. Clearly her presence here in the French court was seen as toxic by Toulouse, but Louis was still too ill to make a decision on her future. Camden Place was a beautiful house with high ceilings and picture windows, fine ornaments, and every imaginable comfort – but now it was just her prison. Members of the court, who had previously been her colleagues, now shunned her. She stared out the window but there was no light, no glimmer of hope. She still yearned to find her son, and she was missing William. He seemed like the only person in the world who cared about her. The room was cold and damp, even in the height of summer. Sleep seemed unlikely so she decided on some action. Anything to break the monotony and boredom.

Checking to see if the coast was clear she stepped out of her bedroom into the main corridor. Then tiptoed down the stairs to the servants' quarters. Luckily all the doors were unlocked, and nobody was about. Soon the servants would be up and at it, preparing the house for the day ahead, but at this moment she was alone. So, she walked into the servants' room and over to a pile of old yellowing newspapers in the corner. Taking a few of these, she quietly returned to her room.

There was a coal scuttle in the bedroom, also lucifers' for lighting the candles

She set about tearing up the newspaper to set a fire in the hearth. The thought of a glowing hot fire cheered her.

Then an odd thing happened; just as she was tearing the first few pieces, a story in the paper caught her eye. It was from *The Times* and two weeks old. The article was about the deaths of a well-known local businessman in Gravesend, John Bennett, and the captain of the *Spirit of Rochester*, John Lynch. Both were killed in a tragic accident while walking to the Excise office, being hit by an out of control brewers' dray. The driver of the dray, Jessie Armitage, was in hospital with serious injuries.

Marie read the article again and again. So, they were dead. But there was no mention of William, or anyone else she knew. It was too much of a coincidence for this to be an accident. She knew she must contact Gordon immediately to find out what had occurred, and if there was any news of Pierre. She would have liked to send a telegram to William but had no address for him. There was no option other than to take matters into her own hands.

Marie put on her strongest, most weatherproof coat, and slipped out of the bedroom.

She walked down the grand staircase and then slipped out through one of the back doors. The house had a long driveway through parkland, with high ornamental gates to keep intruders out. Marie guessed these might be locked so instead went across the parkland and squeezed through a gap in the perimeter fence, probably made by the local children. She then walked through the pouring rain, down the country lane, to the village post office. It was still too early, and not open, so she waited under the covered lichgate of the adjacent churchyard, until it was. As soon as the post office opened she walked in and dictated a telegram addressed to Gordon, at New Tavern Fort, imploring him to give her some information on what was happening. Having completed her mission, she returned to the house, retracing her steps so that her temporary escape would not be noticed.

Gordon got the telegram that Saturday afternoon. He did not want Marie involved but knew that sooner or later she had to be allowed to see her Pierre. Though whether the boy would recognise her would be another matter. He then telegrammed William in London.

*

It was with some relief therefore, that late on that wretched Saturday afternoon, a telegram boy arrived with news from Gordon. It was an invitation to meet him at New Tavern Fort on Monday. It was the news I had been waiting for.

*

I arrived back at the fort, at the appointed time on the Monday morning. Gordon greeted me coolly; he was clearly still preoccupied. We went into his office and he explained the situation to date.

'Thanks for coming back Reeves. I am sorry to say things have not cooled off since you left. The town is rife with rumour. I have also received a telegram from this Marie woman, asking about your whereabouts and if there is any news on Pierre. It is a good thing our security here at the fort is good, or we would be besieged by journalists trying to find a story.'

I said nothing and let Gordon continue. 'We have Police Inspector Daniels coming to see you this morning. Straightforward sort of fellow. Just give him nothing to chew on. If he pushes as to why you have spent so much time in Gravesend, tell him you have been doing special assignments for myself, but you cannot reveal what they are – as they are militarily sensitive. Got that? Same if he mentions Lynch, Bennett or Armitage – say as little as possible.'

I nodded. 'Thank you Gordon for your help with this but what I really want to know is how Pierre is doing?' Gordon sighed slightly and adjusted his sitting position. 'I am afraid the news is not good. He is now in hospital just outside Dartford, in a room by himself. It seems his physical health is improving, albeit only gradually, but his mental condition is, shall we say, delicate.'

'I would like to visit him as soon as possible and with Marie by my side.'

Gordon's face dropped at this. 'I think that would be unwise. The boy is not ready yet and the situation here is too fragile.'

'I must insist. Marie has a right to know her son is alive. I will be discreet and keep her away from here. I will also keep her identity secret at the hospital.'

We sat in silence for a few moments. Finally, Gordon relented. 'Very well. So be it. But be careful. You have much to lose if word of this gets out.'

I stood up, shook his hand, and left the room.

Within minutes I was walking into town to send a telegram to Chislehurst. The contents of my message were a problem. What do you tell someone when their child is safe after being lost, possibly dead, for almost a year? Finally, I decided to keep it business-like, and simply inform her of the facts. That I hoped we could meet tomorrow at Gravesend station at 10 a.m. from where I would take her in a horse and carriage, to the hospital where he was being cared for.

Simple stuff, but my hand was shaking as I handed my note to the telegraph office clerk. I gave my address as the Eagle, as I wanted to keep all publicity away from Gordon.

I then walked back down to the Eagle, and booked in. Sam seemed glad to see me again and had my old room available. Having organised this, I went back to the fort for my interview with Police Constable Daniels. He soon arrived and was much as I expected, old school, stiff and humourless. He did a lot of writing into his notebook. I sat and answered his questions without saying very much at all. Clearly the police were suspicious but the seafaring community in Gravesend had already adopted a wall of silence around Lynch and Bennett's death, so unless a motive could be proved, Armitage might well get off scot free. Which suited me.

*

At Camden Place, my telegram had been received and scrutinised by Toulouse. After deciding on what action he thought appropriate, he took it into the ailing Emperor's bedroom and discussed the contents with Louis Napoleon himself. Marie was then summoned to the drawing room for a private meeting with Toulouse, which the Emperor would not attend.

Marie entered the room looking as well turned out as always. Toulouse stood in front of her. 'Thank you Marie for meeting me. I have some news, which you may find more than acceptable.' Marie stood nervous, vulnerable, her outer persona crumbling. 'What is it?' she said.

Toulouse fingered the telegram in his hand and took his time to answer. 'Good news – your son, Pierre, has been found. It seems that Mr Reeves is to thank for this.'

Marie almost swooned at that moment. Seeing this, Toulouse reached over and caught her as she tipped forward. 'Now, now madame. Please sit yourself down. Clearly this is too much for you.' He then helped her into an armchair. She could not contain her excitement. 'Is he well? Has he been injured?'

Toulouse sighed. 'I'm sorry, the telegram only gives the briefest of facts. However, Mr Reeves does want to meet you at Gravesend station tomorrow, from where he will take you to be reunited with Pierre.'

Marie sat staring back, trying to find the right words. She stuttered, 'And it will be alright for me to leave the house and go to Gravesend?'

Toulouse gave a greasy smile. 'Of course.'

Marie smiled; this was her dream come true. 'I will bring Pierre back to the house, so that Louis can see he is alive and well?'

At this, Toulouse's demeanour changed. 'I have briefly discussed the contents of the telegram with the Emperor. Whilst we welcome the news, we do not feel that it is appropriate for Pierre to live in this house with you.'

There was a stunned silence. 'But why?' Marie implored.

Toulouse seemed to enjoy his next statement, his lips making the most of every word. 'Let us be frank Marie. I know that in the past, the Emperor has been fond of you. There was even talk that Pierre might be his son.'

'Pierre is his son!'

Toulouse was not going to allow this to break his flow. 'The problem is that the rumour has been a cause of upset to the Empress Eugenie. Louis feels that seeing Pierre around the house might be upsetting to his wife. So, we are both minded that you should leave the court and return to France.'

Marie was speechless. Toulouse less so. 'Obviously, we would see that you were financially secure and would find you a residence in Paris, where you and Pierre could start a new life.'

'What if I said no?'

Toulouse sighed. 'I am afraid that would not be acceptable. If you do not agree to these terms, then I will put you under house arrest. You will not keep your rendezvous with this Mr Reeves, and he will assume you do not want to know. Then at a later date we will escort you back to France. Have I made myself clear?'

Marie was crestfallen but she knew that Pierre must come first. 'Very well. I will meet my son tomorrow and we will travel on to Paris. You have got what you wanted.'

Toulouse brought his fingertips together; the meeting was over, he smiled. 'Splendid. Please pack a bag. I will provide any necessary paperwork for the voyage. That will be all.'

At that he clicked his heels and walked out of the room. Marie went back to her bedroom and reluctantly prepared for her departure.

*

I returned to the Eagle later that afternoon and soon had a telegram boy bringing me news from Camden Place. Yes, Marie was delighted and would be at the station as arranged.

I was thrilled beyond measure. I returned to the fort to look up Asif, who now appeared to be a permanent fixture at the garrison. He was pleased to see me, as I him. Gordon also lent us the engineer's stagecoach and four horses, which Asif could drive if need be.

I could hardly sleep that night. I hoped that Marie felt the same. Dawn broke. The sun shone. I walked to the fort and got onto the footplate of the carriage alongside the smiling Asif. All was well. It was time to meet Marie again.

PART 4

Journey Home

THIRTY-FIVE

The Hospital

We parked the horses and carriage outside Gravesend station. It was nearly 10 a.m. and the town was buzzing with activity. I left Asif in charge of the horses and waited on the platform for the train from London. I felt very anxious about the day ahead, but I knew that I must see this through. All common sense went out the window when Marie was involved, she had that hold on me. I waited patiently, time dragged on, I looked again at my pocket watch. Finally, I could see the smoke from the engine as the train emerged from the deep chalk gorge into which the rail line is set. It trundled to a halt alongside the platform. I waited a few moments for the smoke to disperse – and there she was. I had to stop myself running towards her, but instead tried a nonchalant stroll. She was on her own. Beautifully dressed as always. Beautiful as always. She was wearing the deep maroon skirt she had worn when we first met, and as usual her hair was tied immaculately into a bun, with her dark hair contrasting with the white blouse that came up to her neckline.. All as well. Only one surprise, she had a heavy bag with her that the porter was helping her take off the train. I tipped the porter and picked it up myself, it was indeed quite heavy.

I smiled. Her gentle small hand reached out and I bowed down and kissed her fingertips. She looked at me and spoke softly. 'Is it true William? You have found my boy?'

I stood up and looked into her eyes. 'Yes, Marie, we have done it. He is alive.'

She seemed almost overcome and for a moment I thought she might swoon. Finally getting herself back together and dabbing a tear from her eye, she replied, 'Thank you, thank you so much. I never thought this day would come.'

I just stood there staring at her. The train was now departing, and noise and smoke filled the air for a few seconds. Then all was quiet again. 'I have to tell you Marie that although Pierre is safe, he is unwell, so he has been taken to a hospital.'

'How unwell, is he going to die? I could not stand that.'

I gently took her arm and slowly walked her off the platform. 'No, he is not going to die but he will need much care. I have a horse and carriage with me, and Asif to drive. We can visit him in hospital now. If that is what you wish?' She nodded in the affirmative. We walked arm in arm out of the station to the waiting carriage, no small talk was needed, just like an old married couple, happy in our own company. At the carriage, Asif effortlessly lifted her case onto the roof rack. Marie thanked him for his help. Then I helped her into the carriage and sat beside her. I had already discussed the route with him. The hospital was located about five miles west of Gravesend, just off the London Road, in Dartford. We set off.

Strangely now we were sitting so close together it almost felt awkward. I did not know if this was the appropriate moment to tell Marie how much I had missed her, how I still longed for her. But no, that was too soon. We had to reunite Marie with her son first, that would be emotion enough for one day! So, we spoke about normal things, how the French court was doing in Chislehurst, Napoleon's gall bladder problems and how they affected her position in the household. Then we went on to talk about how Pierre had been discovered, the condition he was in. Clearly this cast a shadow over her happiness. I myself was concerned at the state the boy would be in when we reached the hospital. I tried to keep these doubts to myself.

The carriage clattered along the London road towards Dartford for almost an hour before we pulled off and entered a side road. Asif drew the horses to a stop. I looked out and there before me were the gates of the hospital, with the inscription 'City of London Lunatic Asylum' and below that the year, presumably of its opening, '1866'. I could see out of the corner of my eye that Marie had also seen the sign.

'William, what is this? It says lunatic asylum; you have brought my boy to this?'

I was also dumbfounded. I could not believe my own stupidity – I had not bothered to ask Gordon the details. I had just relied on Asif to get us here quickly and without fuss. I scratched around for suitable words. 'I think it must have been the only hospital available. I'm sure all will be well inside.' Then shouted to Asif, 'Carry on. Drive us up to the porter's office.'

Marie sunk back into her seat; it was as if she had been slapped in the face. We parked the carriage outside the porter's office, and I went inside to sort out the procedure for seeing Pierre. The porter was a gruff old fellow with mutton chop sideburns and not much hair on top. His reddened face showed a poor choice of diet or too much time spent in alehouses. He offered to take us to the boy. I went back to the carriage and helped Marie out. We looked about us. The hospital itself was a fine modern building, built in the Gothic style and surrounded by landscaped gardens. This good experience seemed to calm Marie. I turned to Asif. 'Can you look after the horses? I'm taking Marie in.'

At that I took her by the arm and entered the hospital. The porter was clearly impressed that such an attractive and well-dressed woman was visiting and immediately became much more helpful. He took us out of his office then down an immensely long corridor. I could tell Marie was apprehensive. The porter spoke in effusive tones.

'This is a marvellous building. Even the corridors are specially built; long and wide, so you can walk for hours, even when it is raining outside. A lot of the lunatics like walking.'

The word 'lunatic' seemed to hit Marie like a hammer. I gestured for her to say nothing. We carried on. As we got deeper into the bowels of the hospital the noise of the inmates became louder; shouting, hollering, crying, repeating words again and again. We passed one of them, who was pissing up a wall. The porter stopped and clipped his ear. 'Get on with you. If I see you doing that again, you'll be locked in.' The lunatic looked back with blank eyes. We all moved on. Finally, at the end of the corridor there was a small ward to our left. The porter pointed. 'There he is, the French boy. Anything else I can do for you?'

He stood, unmoving, I got the hint and put a crown into his hand.

'Thank you sir, you know where I am if you need help.'

At that he departed back down the long corridor.

We looked into the small ward, thankfully it only had one bed, and in it was Pierre – no doubt of that. Marie had finally got to see her son. She raced into the room and was about to throw her arms around him, then she hesitated. Yes, it was definitely Pierre, but his eyes looked dead. There seemed to be no recognition that the woman coming towards him with open arms was his mother. He was just lying in bed, chewing a sheet, staring, mumbling incoherently. Marie turned to me. 'What has happened to him? What have you done?'

I could say nothing, my hopes for a joyous reunion between mother and son were in tatters. She reached over and gently touched her boy's forehead. Still no sign of life, no reaction. 'Pierre, it is me, I've come for you.' At that she sat on the bed and tried to hug him. It was sad, almost pathetic to watch. Still little reaction ensued from the boy. She sat back on the bed clearly distraught and lost for words. 'What has happened William, why has this happened?'

I was as concerned as her but had no answers.

'I don't know; I can only guess that all those months incarcerated in an underground cell have severely affected his mental health. I had no idea he was this bad.' We were in silence for a few seconds unable to say anything; the silence was rudely broken by some furious banging on the door – it was one of the patients shouting and hollering about nothing. A few seconds later an orderly arrived and dragged them away, screaming. Marie looked at me, her eyes welling up with sadness. 'We must get him out of here. Get him back to things he might remember, things that will heal his soul.'

We spent several minutes by his bedside, hoping, praying for some sign of recognition. Nothing occurred, just a blank face staring back at us. Finally, Marie seemed to make up her mind. She kissed Pierre on his forehead and said quietly, 'We will be back for you Pierre. We will take you away from here and bring you home.'

At that she made to leave. I touched her arm. 'Is that wise Marie? Is he ready?' She was clearly not in the mood for discussion. 'Come, let us find what paperwork needs to be done to get him released from this hellhole.'

She then virtually marched down the corridor and back to the porter's office. If Marie had her way we would have dragged Pierre out there and then, but clearly there were procedures. I persuaded her to go outside and sit in the carriage while I talked to the porter. She agreed. The porter clearly felt his job was not to be too helpful, but I ascertained that a letter from the person who had originally sent Pierre to the hospital, and was paying his keep, Gordon, was required to get his release. It also appeared that release could take place immediately the said letter of authority was produced. I thanked him, bade farewell, and stepped back into the waiting carriage.

'We need a letter of authority from Gordon to legally remove him.' She seemed alright with this.

'Then let us get back to Gravesend now and get this sorted.' I agreed to this course of action and within seconds the coach was out through the gates, heading east along the London road.

THIRTY-SIX

The Journey Home

WITHIN THE HOUR WE HAD arrived back in Gravesend and I let Marie off at the Eagle, then proceeded on to the fort. Luckily, Gordon was in, so I was able to appraise him of the situation. With a heavy heart he wrote out a letter on headed paper giving me permission to remove Pierre from the hospital. I could tell from his demeanour that he was now tired of this whole affair. I left him in his office and returned to the Eagle with his letter in my pocket.

Marie had made herself at home in my room. She seemed both elated at her son's reappearance but sad about his condition, and fearful of what the future might hold. She gently took my hand and sat me on the bed.

'Was Gordon alright about removing Pierre from the asylum?'

I nodded and showed her the letter of intent. 'Thank you so much William, I owe you everything.'

She then gently put her arms around my shoulders and hugged me. She continued, 'But I have something to tell you. I am no longer welcome at the French court at Camden Place. I must return to France.'

I decided that talk was for later on. I looked into her eyes and kissed her full on the lips. She responded in kind and we were soon together on the bed. All the problems of the day, all the horrors of the lunatic asylum, were swept away. In the bedroom Marie was a different person – younger, softer, nicer. She could shut the world out and invite you into her magic kingdom. And that she did.

Sometime later I reluctantly got out of bed and dressed. We were both now hungry so went downstairs into the bar. I knew the food here was indifferent, but we were both in such a good mood that nothing could spoil things. I turned to her. 'Let me come with you to France. The three of us, we could set up home in Paris. What do you think?'

She seemed both touched and surprised. 'William, that is so kind of you, but what would you do in a foreign country?'

'I'd do the same as I do here, private investigations, journalism. I know it would take me a while to learn the language, but we could get there together.'

She looked both happy and perturbed by my answer. 'I think you underestimate the difficulties William. You have a life here – would you really be willing to give it all up for me?'

I smiled. 'Yes, without hesitation.'

She gently touched my hand. 'Let us see what tomorrow brings. This is such a big decision, perhaps we both need to sleep on it.'

And so, the conversation ended, and we had a simple meal of bread and cheese before returning to our room.

Such was my passion for Marie we got little sleep that night. I could tell she felt the same. Both of us were half awake, waiting for dawn to break. This was a big day in our lives; we both knew it.

At 7 a.m. I left Marie and headed for the fort. Asif was already up with the horses fed, watered, and groomed. He took the leads, and we headed off down West Street, picking up Marie at the Eagle's front door. It was another fine morning. The London road was clear of traffic and we made steady progress.

By nine o'clock we were back at the gates of the asylum. Marie and I left the stagecoach, leaving Asif in charge. At the office we saw the same grizzly porter as we did yesterday. I showed him the letter from Gordon and he dolefully showed us through to Pierre's bedroom. Clearly nothing had changed. I also noted that the lad had wet the bed. Pierre seemed oblivious of his own urine and lay comatose in a foetal potion on the bedspread, chewing his thumb. I addressed the porter.

'We will be taking him to another hospital. We do not think this asylum is suitable for his requirements.'

The man seemed indifferent. 'You're welcome to him,' were his only words. Then he left us and presumably returned to his office.

We were now left with Pierre.

Marie scrabbled to get him out of bed and dressed.

I stood by, fairly useless. No sense was coming from the boy. Just animal noises. No recognition of his mother. Despite this Marie did not lose her cool. She stuck to the task. Finally, we had him dressed and I collected his meagre belongings. We then half walked; half dragged him along the long corridor. All the while there was an endless backdrop of mindless shouting and swearing from the other inmates.

It was with relief that we got out of the asylum, into the warm sunshine and put Pierre into the coach. Marie sat alongside him. With the boy settled, she called out through the window, 'Can we go straight to Dover?'

I looked at the ever-patient Asif, he looked at me. I felt duty bound to tell her that it would be a long day's drive.

'Marie, that will be a good ten-hour journey, are you sure?'

'Yes, it will be too difficult getting Pierre on and off trains. Let us ride down to the ferry at Dover.'

I nodded to Asif. 'Very well, let us get moving.' At that he whipped the horses into life, and we set off down the old London road heading for the coast.

I knew the old coaching route from memory, although these days I usually took the train if travelling to Dover. The route followed the old Roman road, Watling Street – Gravesend, Higham, Rochester Bridge, Faversham, Canterbury, Dover. There were numerous coaching inns en route where the horses could be fed and watered. I had no exact idea what times the mail packets sailed, but hopefully we should make Dover before sunset, and get the last ferry to Boulogne before nightfall.

The route was not without its pleasant diversions, with the white chalk pits etched into the hillsides towering above the distant Thames. This countryside then gave way to the softer, lusher landscapes of rural Kent. We passed over the River Medway at Rochester Bridge – and I could see to my left the meandering stretch of river at Strood, where I had been stabbed by John Bennett. Then onwards through Rochester high street itself, with its fine castle and cathedral. All should have been well, but a strange feeling of unease gripped me. I could not put my finger on it but eventually it came; the weather was turning. It was changing from bright sunshine to dull and heavy. And the humidity was building. Even sitting on top, with the wind in my hair I could feel the closeness gathering. Below us, inside the coach all seemed to be going well. Pierre was just sitting quietly, his eyes dead to the world, but at least Marie could now relax slightly. By the time we reached the hop fields of Faversham the humidity was noticeable, a clamminess prevailed. There must be a storm coming, and a big one at that.

The day wore on. We had to push the horses hard. Stops at coaching inns were perfunctory affairs – food and water for the horses and little time for anything else, then back on the road. I marvelled at how the Royal Mail coach drivers did this day in day out, as I was already getting tired. The wind was now in our faces, driving from the south – from the English Channel itself.

We rode through Canterbury, hardly noticing the beautiful cathedral, then dipped southwards, going through the sparsely populated open chalk downlands. We made one final stop at the Bell Inn at Lyddon. I could tell Asif had noticed the humidity as he threw a bucket of water over the sweating horses. I asked Marie if she was alright and she nodded. She had no wish to leave the coach, clearly she was nervous of anything which might cause Pierre to become excitable or restless.

Standing alongside the horses, I turned to Asif. 'The wind is strengthening and changing direction. It is coming from the south-west now. Will that make the crossing choppier?'

He was clearly concerned. 'The English Channel, very narrow at Dover, bad storm, no good.' We left it at that and got back onto the coach and drove on.

Finally, Dover came into view, it was now early evening and the light was getting odder by the minute. We passed Crabble Mill, on its outskirts, and weaved down the cobbled streets of this growing town. Then finally we got a glimpse of the sea ahead. The English Channel. Somewhere beyond that was the French coast but the heavy cloud obscured any view of that.

We took the coach down to the road alongside Dover Town station, where it was a short walk to the ferry terminal dock on Admiralty Pier. Asif skilfully stopped the horses, who were by now only too grateful for a rest. We were all tired, but the sight in front of us gave us no comfort. Crowds were milling around, mostly people who had come off the train. Leaving Asif in charge, I walked over to the ferry dock entrance. A uniformed man with a strong moustache stood there arguing with a few irritated travellers.

'I'm sorry ladies and gentlemen. There will be no more ferries tonight. Due to bad weather, all crossings are cancelled until further notice.'

There was much displeasure from the waiting crowd, but I could see his reasoning. The winds were now westerly and must be racing down the channel and squeezing through the straits of Dover. Beyond the wind there was the ever-present threat of a violent storm. When this storm broke, it was going to be vicious, and a boat on the English Channel was no place to be. I walked back to the coach and told everyone the news. Asif was not perturbed but Marie was clearly desperate. Was this a sign from God? We had come all this way but could not get out of the country, yet.

I quickly thought about my memories of Dover from a previous trip. There was a good hotel alongside the town station on the seafront, the Lord Warden Hotel. We could try and stay the night there. I told them of my idea and as there was no alternative, they agreed. It was a fine building with views over the harbour and Admiralty Pier. As I dismounted from the coach, I could feel the first raindrops on my collar. I went inside to talk to the receptionist. Clearly many more people wanted to stay the night because of the adverse weather, so I could only obtain one room in the hotel proper. There were also some quarters at the back where the servants could sleep and stable their horses.

I decided to give Marie and Pierre the hotel room, and I would sleep in the servants' quarters with Asif. I returned to the coach and all agreed that was a good course of action. We were all by now so tired and fearful of this cruel weather that to find lodgings at this hour was a comfort in itself.

Within half an hour all was resolved. Marie and Pierre had been settled into their bedroom on the ground floor and myself, Asif and the horses were sorted out with our overnight accommodation in the servants' sleeping quarters. Getting Pierre out of the carriage and through reception had not been too difficult. I had told the clerk on reception that the boy was a simpleton but that his mother would make sure there was no trouble. He seemed to accept this without query.

The rest of the evening was spent quietly, while the thunder rolled on outside we kept our heads down. Marie had food sent to her room. I ate in the servants' quarters. They were a rough and ready lot down there, but not too concerned about a gentleman in their midst. I simply explained it away by saying the hotel was full, which was a half-truth, anyway.

The sleeping arrangements though, were less successful. Myself and Asif were together in the same damp basement dormitory, which smelt musty, at best. Outside I could still hear the storm worsening. Inside, the snoring and farting of my bedfellows made it impossible to sleep. I was also very worried about the future. A whole new life in France – an idea both exhilarating and frightening at the same time. Small wonder sleep deserted me. I noticed Asif was fine though, he could sleep anywhere. I was also worried sick about Marie. Would Pierre be alright? Would he have nightmares? Wet the bed? Have a screaming fit? Finally, I gave in to my concerns. Around midnight I crept out of the dormitory, sliding past my smelly sleeping compatriots. I quietly tiptoed my way into the hotel proper and found the porter still on reception. He was half asleep but recognising me, soon perked up. I explained that I was travelling with Marie and her disabled son and that I had forgotten to give them some particularly important medicines. The porter was not having it at first, but a gold sovereign slipped into his hand did the trick. I got the key and quietly walked up to their room.

I gently unlocked the door and making no noise, went into the room. I could see Marie on the bed asleep. On a second bed I could see a bundle of bedclothes, so assumed Pierre was asleep underneath. I gingerly crept up to Marie's bed and slipped under the bedclothes. I breathed a sigh of relief; I had got in without waking her! Just to be near her was still magical to me. I could feel the warmth of her naked body, the slight smell of her lingering perfume. I was happy just to lay there taking this all in, as outside the storm rattled the windowpanes.

We stayed like this for a while, then she rolled over and bumped into me. Her eyes opened with a start. She barely had let out the word 'William' when a worry crossed her forehead. She looked around the room. There was no other sound. She quickly and effortlessly got out of bed and went over to where Pierre was sleeping. The bed was empty.

THIRTY-SEVEN

The Raging Sea

MARIE STOOD STUNNED, UNABLE TO speak. I could see the look of total panic on her face. She ran over to the window, which was half open. From here to the walkway below was just a few feet and if Pierre had been careful and avoided the cast-iron railings, he could have got away easily.

She looked at me with hopelessness in her eyes. 'William, he has gone. Where do we start to look for him? What do we do?'

I almost shrugged at this point. In truth he could now be anywhere. Why hadn't we made sure the window was locked, or that the room was not on the ground floor?

I stared out over the harbour, scanning the promenade and pier. Then something amazing happened. A flash of lightning illuminated the whole of the seascape in front of us. For a brief moment the whole area was floodlit with the cruel yellow light of a lightning flash. And there he was, standing on Admiralty Pier, perhaps a furlong away. I could swear to it. I pointed for Marie's sake. 'Look, out over there. Standing on the pier.'

She stared into the distance and could just make out the figure of her boy. Then the light was gone and in a few seconds the thunder rolled in. The noise was deafening. This was one humdinger of a storm – and Pierre was in the middle of it!

Admiralty Pier was where the railway line terminated, and the steam packets moored up. It was a large stone breakwater along which ran the railway line. It was not the place to be when a storm was raging and the waves from an angry sea were crashing into the stonework. I urged Marie to get dressed. We needed to get down to the pier now. Marie pulled on an underskirt and stopped at that.

'I don't have time William. I'll go out as I am.'

At this we speedily departed the room scarcely shutting the door behind us. We clattered down the corridor and past the porter, I yelled at him. 'Our boy has wandered off onto the harbour wall, can you call for men to help us save him?' He looked at me blankly. I didn't have time to stop and explain further. I turned to Marie.

'I'll get Asif, and some rope. If he falls into the harbour in this weather, he will have no chance.'

At the main door Marie left me, she was almost running now, straight ahead towards the pier. I ran over to the servants' quarters and woke Asif.

'Quick, Asif. Pierre is on the harbour wall. Get the spare rope from the carriage and join me there.' He was quickly on the case and heading for the stabling block. I turned and rushed back towards the harbour breakwater.

The thunderstorm was still at its height, the rain beating down. I could see Marie ahead of me, her white pantaloon undergarments already sodden and her shoeless feet slipping over the greasy wet flagstones of the pier. I caught up with her and put my hand on her shoulder.

'Don't worry we will get him. Asif is bringing some rope.' At that I fell silent. With the rain in our faces we were struggling to make progress, we were moving forward at a desperate half walk, half stumble. We finally reached the spot on the pier where I had seen Pierre. Without the lightning flash I would never have spotted him in a million years.

The pier was a substantial affair with flagstones above a concrete base, rising perhaps fifteen feet in height above the waterline. The railway line was on the north side of the breakwater so should have been immune to waves crashing from the south-west. However, such was the force of the storm that the sea was constantly breaking over and swamping the railway track, and the narrow path alongside it. Iron railings should have kept anyone walking alongside the railway track safe, but the raging sea was making a mockery of man's engineering achievement – constantly rising and falling and sucking anything and anybody into its grasp.

So, holding her hand tightly, and with the other hand grasping the iron railings, we gingerly made our way towards the boy. Every few seconds the waves broke over the breakwater and soaked us. But we managed to stay on our feet and keep going.

There was another savage streak of lightning and we could see Pierre ahead. Still in the same position, about fifty yards away – just standing still, looking at the raging sea. No other help had arrived yet, though through the light of the flash I could see Asif just leaving the promenade and heading up the breakwater in our direction.

We kept going until we were about twenty yards short of Pierre. Something about his demeanour suggested we must be careful in our actions. Marie shouted at him imploringly in French, 'Pierre, please, stay absolutely still. We will get you.'

For a few seconds we all froze.

Pierre turned his head towards us. He looked at his mother for a moment, smiled slightly, then to our horror – he jumped! Straight into the raging sea!

I looked at Marie, she was mortified. There was no choice. I ran to where he had been standing and jumped in. I hit the water so hard, it was like hitting a brick wall. It was freezing, bitter. All the air came out of my lungs. For a few moments I had to fight the panic, then my heartbeat calmed just enough to think straight. I paddled furiously but could not see any sign of him. I looked above me, and Marie was standing there. She pointed to my right. I looked, and looked, but I could see nothing. Then to my horror, she jumped in! There and then – in her soggy white pantaloons! She hit the water hard and like me was clearly winded and disorientated. I followed my instinct and half swam, half paddled, to where she was struggling. But it was already too late, her head was under the water, she was in a state of total desperation. I grabbed her around the waist, trying to hoist her head above the waves so she could breathe, but her panic was beating us both. At this rate she would take me down with her. The waves were so strong, they beat us both back against the breakwater stone. For a moment I thought I might be able to hold onto the slippery rock, but the ebb and flow of the raging tide sucked us both back out into the maelstrom.

I was close to giving up hope. I was just not strong enough for this, we were both doomed. Then above me, I heard a voice. It was Asif, with a rope. He caught my eye and gesturing, threw it towards me. Three or four times he missed but finally I had grabbed it. I was still holding Marie desperately, my fingernails embedded into her body. Somehow, in some way, Asif pulled us towards him. Using my free hand, I scrabbled at the stone, half my body out of the water. By sheer force of will, and great strength, Asif got us out of the water, under the railings, and onto the flat stonework alongside the rail track. Marie was by now a dead weight. I could not tell if she had taken in too much water or hit her head against the rock, but she was virtually unconscious.

I touched Asif's outstretched hand and mouthed, 'Thank you.'

I looked back below us to the sea.

There was no sign of the boy.

Nothing.

I looked again at Asif and his face told me what I knew. We would never see the lad alive again. Strangers had now arrived to see if they could help and were now gathered around Marie's prostrate body. She looked awful. White faced. While others watched, Asif acted, putting her on to her side and squeezing the water out of her lungs. I pummelled her back hoping that would push the seawater out. For a few seconds nothing happened, then, thank God, it did. She vomited up water and debris. She was frozen and hurt, but still alive. Blood was also coming out freely from a vicious cut on her forehead.

We managed to get her sitting up and I pressed a handkerchief on the wound. She was clearly beyond exhaustion but found the strength to speak.

'William, have you found him? Have you got my boy?'

I looked into her eyes and indicated that we had not.

'I'm so sorry Marie, he is gone. I never saw him again after he left the pier.'

She looked both angry and hysterical in equal measures. 'Go on in, keep going, you must find him. I implore you!'

I looked at Asif, he shook his head. I turned to her. 'I'm so sorry, there is nothing more we can do. The sea is too strong and cold, he will be dead by now.'

She scowled at me. 'Cowards, miserable English cowards.' Then realising her hopelessness, she burst into tears. I put my arms around her and with the help of the others, got her to her feet.

One of the strangers then said, 'We must get out of here; this is too dangerous. We could all get swept away by the waves.'

Marie's face showed a sense of total desolation but unable to walk unaided, we led her back down the breakwater path to the safety of the promenade.

We all made it safely and waiting there was a hospital carriage. We gladly accepted the help and took her to the local hospital.

THIRTY-EIGHT

The Funeral

WE STAYED IN DOVER THAT week. Marie's head wound was not as bad as feared and she was able to be released from Buckland Hospital. She did not want to carry on staying at the Lord Warden – the view of the pier from her window brought back nightmares of that awful night. So, we moved to a more modest hotel in the town centre, near to Dover Priory station. We slept the next few nights at that hotel.

Poor Pierre's body was washed up on Dover's pebble beach, on the next morning's tide. We had no idea how long it would take for the coroner to release the corpse for burial. It seemed petty to keep Asif away from his work in Gravesend any longer, there was also the cost of stabling and feed for the horses to consider, so with a heavy heart I asked Asif if he could take the carriage back to Gravesend. As always he obliged without complaint.

There were now just the two of us. We spent the next few days walking the promenade, looking out to sea. On sunny days we could see the French coast, almost within touching distance. Marie was distant and preoccupied. Distraught over her boy's death. She took to wearing black widow's weeds most of the time. She was clearly unsure of the future, as was I. On days when the sun shone I tried broaching the subject of our future, but it felt awkward, strained. Would we still move to Paris, or stay in England? The one thing she did seem intent on was not returning to Camden Place.

The coroner released the body for burial in less than a week, but it felt like a lifetime. He had pronounced that the cause of Pierre's death was drowning while his mind was disturbed. It was an open and shut case.

It was clearly impractical to take the corpse to France for burial, and Marie had no desire to beg Napoleon for the permission to have him buried in Chislehurst.

As luck would have it, the hotel manager's brother was well connected to a church in the town centre of Dover – it was St Peters and St Pauls Church, in the Charlton area. We visited the church together, and though we had no connection to the town, the vicar kindly allowed us a burial in the churchyard. Perhaps the name of the church was apt, as St Peter was the patron saint of fishermen.

Young Pierre would not have been the first, nor the last person drowning in the English Channel to be buried there. I telegrammed Gordon to let him know the arrangements and enquired as to the health of Asif and Jessie Armitage. I got no response so assumed he was away from Gravesend.

The day of the funeral dawned. I paid for it myself. It was the least I could do. Sadly, it was the coldest, greyest day imaginable, even though it was the height of summer. The body was taken in a hearse behind a black horse, with black feathered head decoration, from the mortuary to the church. It was a fine old Gothic church, slightly away from the busiest part of town but within yards of the River Dour. We followed the hearse in a black hansom cab. There was just the two of us due – the only other people at the funeral would be the vicar and pallbearers.

The undertakers carried the coffin in through the old timber doors of the church and along the aisle. At that moment I caught sight of my dearest comrades – Gordon along with Asif, sitting alone in the empty church. I nodded. Asif smiled. Gordon gave the briefest of nods in return.

The ceremony progressed. What could be said of Pierre's life? He should now have been looking forward to manhood in Paris. But the war and the greed of men had stopped all that. The only crumb of comfort was that he was getting a Christian burial, and not just rotting away in a tunnel under a pub in Gravesend.

Marie was impassive throughout. Her grief was difficult to touch, or imagine, so for the most part I kept my distance. English reserve, or cowardice?

The service ended and the coffin was carried out. I took the front corner and Asif the other, with the undertakers carrying the rear.

Outside the day had gone from grey damp to howling wind and rain. We carried on regardless. What else was there to do? Soon we were off the path and standing in sodden grass beside a newly dug grave. A few more words and the coffin was lowered. Marie and I threw some dirt on top of it. The gravedigger then started filling in more dirt as we walked away. I looked over and saw Marie was struggling, so I took her arm to stop her slipping on the wet grass. She looked very distant.

I had hoped that the church graveyard would have a view over the channel, to the boy's homeland of France, but I could see nothing but mist and rain.

After thanking the vicar and undertakers, we went back into the hansom cab. By now we were all cold, wet and thoroughly down. I thanked Gordon and Asif for coming and we all decided to go back to the hotel for a warming drink.

THIRTY-NINE

Farewell to Dover

WE ENTERED THE HOTEL TEAROOMS and I helped Marie into her seat. Gordon also insisted, quite rightly, that Asif join us. Hotels could sometimes be awkward about lascars in their dining rooms but clearly Gordon was a gentleman of stature, and if he was willing to share his table, then the waiting staff had no cause for complaint. I thanked Gordon profusely for coming down to Dover; his response was both measured and warm.

'It is the least we can do in the circumstances. We got the train this morning and will return this afternoon.' He turned to Marie. 'I thought we should let you know how sorry we are for your loss, and ashamed that Pierre's death was due to my fellow countrymen's brutality and avarice.'

She stared back at him, then gently touched his hand with her fingers. 'Thank you.'

Gordon continued, 'Have you made any plans for the future?'

I looked at Marie, she looked at me. We had been avoiding that question all week. I spoke quietly. 'Too soon.' Gordon concurred. I changed the subject.

'Any news on Jessie Armitage?'

Gordon sighed. 'Dead I'm afraid. The injuries were too severe.'

I was saddened by this news.

'That is a shame. At heart he was a good man. What of the deaths of Lynch and Bennett?'

'The formal inquest has yet to take place, but everyone believes that an open verdict is the likely outcome. Just a tragic accident.'

Marie seemed to be concerned at this and spoke up. 'But what of the other men involved? The photographer Mr Bussell, and all the other people who must have known what was happening to those poor boys?'

Gordon was clearly feeling awkward at this and was glad that the waitress brought over a pot of tea at that very moment. We all waited a few moments while teacups were filled, and the waitress departed.

Finally, Gordon replied. 'I'm afraid they are still at large. Also, in all truth if I were to pursue the case against them, it might open up your involvement in the situation. Any link between Napoleon and a senior officer working for our armed forces might be picked up by the press and cause repercussions. I am here in a purely personal capacity. You understand that.'

I replied, 'Of course, and incredibly grateful we are too for your attendance at the funeral.'

I could read from Marie's body language that she was not content with this. Gordon seemed to sense this also.

'Obviously, Reeves, if you returned to Gravesend it might be possible for you to bottom out the remaining threads of this foul undertaking.'

'You mean the child sex ring?'

He looked discomforted by this. 'Indeed.'

There was an awkward silence. Finally, Gordon spoke again.

'So, it is up to you Reeves. You can come back to Gravesend and try and tie up the loose ends, or you can, with my blessing, create a new life wherever you wish.'

And that was the end of the meaningful conversation. Much of the rest of the time was filled with general talk about the awfulness of the weather and quality of the tea and scones served to us. Finally, Gordon and Asif departed for the station. We all stood outside the front door of the hotel; the rain had now abated. I shook their hands warmly. Gordon seemed to have thawed slightly and even gave Marie a little kiss on her outstretched hand.

Then their cab departed, and we were left alone. I knew she was in a delicate state but had to ask her.

'What do you want now Marie? Do you want to return to France? Stay here in England? Please, I need to know.'

She thought for a while then smiled, for the first time in days. 'I think you will not settle in France William; you must return to London and then Gravesend, and finish what you started.'

I looked at her. 'And you. Will you come with me?'

She did not hesitate. 'I will be by your side of course. Tomorrow let us get the train back to London. Our time here is done.'

Perhaps it was my imagination but for the first time that

day the clouds seem to dissipate, and some thin sunshine fell on our faces. 'That is marvellous Marie. Tomorrow will be the start of our new life. Let us go back to the room and prepare for it.' We held hands and walked back into the hotel.

Marie seemed better that night. At times her old self, but those times were still infrequent and passing. There was a sense of loss, not just of Pierre, but of her whole world at Napoleon's court. She looked and behaved like a person sent into exile, no longer a member of the tribe. That worried me no end. Could I compensate for that loss?

Nevertheless, tomorrow dawned and we made ready to leave Dover. Our plan was to take the train back to London, and from there go on to my lodgings in Whitechapel. That would de facto be our first home. I would have gladly asked her to marry me, there and then, but felt inhibited, afraid of doing anything that might scare her away.

So, in the morning we left the hotel and took the short cab journey up to Dover Priory station. We pulled up outside the ticket office. After paying the driver, I walked into the ticket office and bought two tickets for London. We then walked over the footbridge to the London-bound platform. There was still twenty minutes before our train. Marie seemed distant and quiet, so I left her in peace and stood by the platform gate, taking one more look at Dover before we left.

That is when I noticed, sitting awkwardly on the ground with his back propped up against a wall, a beggar. I immediately recognised the uniform he was in and his war medals. He was from the Royal Engineers and had clearly seen service in the Crimea. His military cap, a kepi, was lying on the ground with a few dismal coins in it, and by his side was a scruffy dog. He was dirty, with a scruffy beard, faraway eyes, and a bloodshot red nose. I indicated to Marie that I was just going to speak to him. She smiled at this, then added, 'I must go to the ladies' room. I won't be long.'

At that she set off in a hurry. I hoped all was well with her, but never questioned her on such matters. The beggar turned to me. 'A penny for a smoke gov'?' I looked him up and down. He was scruffy and dirty, but sadly, he was a similar age to me. I reached into my pocket and pulled out a tanner, which I put into his outstretched hand. 'There you are. Get yourself a bite to eat as well.'

He tapped his forehead. 'Thank you gov', God bless you.'

'Were you in Crimea?'

'Royal Engineers I was in; at Sevastopol.'

I smiled. 'I was there as well. Were you involved in the 18th June offensive to break the siege?'

My words were drowned by a locomotive, travelling in the opposite direction. I waited for the smoke and steam to abate and carried on. 'June the 18th 1855, it was the anniversary of Waterloo. Were you there?'

He shook his head. 'I was already gone, a few weeks earlier. Injured, shrapnel in the legs, got sent back to the military hospital in Turkey. It was a shithole that place, if you excuse me language, until that Florence Nightingale turned up. I would be dead without her.'

'What happened to you after that?' I said.

'Sent back to England. Thought the worse was over. Trouble was the wound in my legs hurt so much I could only kill it with drink. That is what has been the death of me. Too much gin. Lost my girl. My home. Now I am just here, getting by as best I can.'

I felt a pang of regret – there were so many veterans like him. But what more could I do?

'I expected to be treated with respect when I got home. That the girls would admire a soldier who had fought for his country. Be in awe of the uniform. But nobody really cared.' He sighed and stroked his dog as he looked at me. 'This is my only real friend. You don't have friends when you have got nothing and nobody. I can see from your suit though that you did alright. Good luck to you, is what I say. Enjoy your life.'

That seemed a fitting end to our conversation. I looked back to the platform, still no sign of Marie. She was taking a long time.

I bade farewell to the old soldier and went back onto the platform. No sign of her. I walked over to the Ladies and tried the door. Though it had a vacant sign up, it was empty. A strange feeling hit the pit of my stomach. I rushed over the footbridge and quickly found the Ladies on the other platform – that was also empty. I was filled with panic. The only answer could be that she jumped on the Dover bound train that had passed through minutes earlier. I ran over to the uniformed platform guard.

'Have you seen a woman, dark hair, dark outfit – getting on the harbour bound train?'

The platform attendant looked at me. 'Yes, she got onto the last train. Only noticed her because not many people travel in that direction. She seemed in a hurry.'

I shouted at him. 'When is the next train leaving from here, going to the harbour?'

He shook his head. 'Not for an hour sir.'

I was gripped by panic. I rushed out of the station, into the road outside. Unbelievably there were no cabs waiting for fares.

I had no choice. I started running down the street, I felt I must get to Dover harbour and try to persuade her to stay.

I ran and ran; I cannot even remember the street names. I just knew I had to keep going downhill, towards the sea and the Admiralty Pier. I was soon exhausted but kept going as best I could. After what felt like hours, but was probably just ten minutes, I was on the seafront heading for the station. I ran along the promenade and reached the station, which was alongside the Lord Warden hotel.

I arrived breathless at the platform. The train from London was already empty and the engine was cooling down. The station was deserted, apart from the station master.

I looked beyond the tracks to Admiralty Pier and the steam packet moored alongside the breakwater. The boat was in full steam. I raced down the pier, on the path alongside the rail track, the flagstones were wet and greasy, but I ignored the danger and ran on.

And then I saw her.

Walking across the gangplank onto the boat.

I tried to yell but was too exhausted, too short of breath.

Within seconds of that, to my horror I could see the crew dragging the empty gangplank onto the boat. With a clunk they slammed shut the gate in the boat's railings. It was too late. I shouted her name. 'Marie.'

Some of the crew and passengers stared at me. Then I knew she had heard. For a moment, she turned, smiled in the way that only she could. Then waved goodbye and disappeared into the crowd. I would never see her again.

 Matador